This book should be returned to any branch of the
Lancashire County Library on or before the date

Lancashire County Library
Bowran Street
Preston PR1 2UX

Lancashire
County Council

www.lancashire.gov.uk/libraries

'O'Brien remains a stunning writer whose career has yet to be properly appreciated ... For any other writer, such a novel might seem brave or even radical. For O'Brien, a grand-dame of literature if ever there was one, it is simply a matter of describing the world, the emotional, fluid, uncontainable world, as she sees it now and always has'   *Sunday Herald*

'O'Brien's new novel finds the author back on sensuous, poetic form'   *Sunday Times*

'This disconcerting and skilfully made book ... a novel that will sound echoes to anyone who has ever been unlucky in love ... a courageous as well as an artful book. It is also a poignant one, whatever its genre, and its shifting, somewhat elusive stance'   *Irish Times*

'Unquestionably great'   *Los Angeles Times*

O'Brien has not lost her ability to sparkle ... *The Light of Evening* is a sensitive and poetic tribute to the author's mother'   *Observer*

'Ireland's greatest female writer ... moving, dark and engrossing'   *Tatler*

In more than twenty books, Edna O'Brien has charted the emotional and psychic landscape of her native Ireland. Often criticized in her own country for her outspoken stance, she has forged a universal audience. Awards and prizes for her work include the Irish PEN Lifetime Achievement Award, Writers' Guild of Great Britain, the Italian Premier Cavour, American National Arts Gold Medal and Ulysses Medal 2006. She grew up in Ireland and now lives in London.

By Edna O'Brien

Edna O'Brien

Girls in their Married Bliss

WEIDENFELD & NICOLSON

A W&N PAPERBACK

First published in Great Britain in 1964
by Jonathan Cape
This paperback edition published in 2007
by Weidenfeld & Nicolson,
an imprint of the Orion Publishing Group Ltd,
Carmelite House, 50 Victoria Embankment,
London EC4Y 0DZ

An Hachette UK company

10 9 8 7 6 5 4

A CIP catalogue record for this book
is available from the British Library.

ISBN 978-0-753-82138-1

Typeset by Input Data Services Ltd, Frome

Printed and bound in Great Britain by
Clays Ltd, St Ives plc

MIX
Paper from
responsible sources
FSC
www.fsc.org   FSC® C104740

www.orionbooks.co.uk

For Ted Allan

1

Not long ago Kate Brady and I were having a few gloomy gin fizzes up London, bemoaning the fact that nothing would ever improve, that we'd die the way we were – enough to eat, married, dissatisfied.

We've always been friends – as kids in Ireland we slept together and I used to push her out of bed on purpose, hoping she'd crack her skull or something. I liked her and all that – I was as jealous as hell of course – but she was too sedate and good, you know that useless kind of goodness, asking people how they are, and how their parents are. At National School she did my compositions for me, and in the Convent of Mercy we clung together because the other eighty girls were even drippier than she, which is saying a lot. When we vamoozed from the convent we went to a linoleum slum in Dublin, and then on to another slum here in London, where, over a period of eighteen months, we got asked out to about three good dinners apiece, which meant six meals for both of us because we had a pact that whoever got asked out would bring back food for the Cinderella. I've ruined the inside of more handbags that way ...

We weren't here a year when she re-met a crank called Eugene Gaillard whom she'd known in Ireland. They took up their old refrain, fell in love, or thought they did and lost no time making puke out of it. The marriage was in the sacristy of a Catholic Church. Question of having to. They wouldn't do it out front because he was divorced and she was heavily pregnant. I was bridesmaid. Pink chiffon and a hat with a veil for which they paid. I looked like the bride. She was in a big, floppy, striped maternity dress and a child's face on her. She's sly, the sort that would look like a child even if she kept her mother in a wardrobe. The priest didn't look towards her stomach once.

When we came out, Eugene drove away very quick, and that shook me because he's the sort of fusser that issues instructions before he lets you into his motor-car. 'Don't step on the running-board, don't push the seat too far back, don't push the other seat too far forwards.' To make himself important. He tore out of the place and down the road like a sportsman. He was laughing too, a thing he doesn't do often.

'What's up?' says I.

'Our Beloved Father is finding a little surprise,' he said, and Kate said, 'What?' just like a wife.

It seems the envelope which he handed to the priest, and which was supposed to contain twenty pounds for marrying them, contained one, orange-coloured, Irish, ten-shilling note, wrapped in several pieces of paper to make the envelope bulky. Well, she flew into a huff and got violet in the face. He told her she was nothing but a farmer's daughter reverting to type, and she told him he was so mean he wouldn't let her buy things for the baby. A dig because he was married before and had kept pram and napkins in storage. He said she had no breeding, and if she wanted to be crude she'd better step out of the car. He said he'd give the twenty pounds to some less pernicious organization and she said, 'Well go on, give it, stop some poor woman and give it to her,' but he sat tight at the wheel and drove with a set purpose to a middling restaurant in Soho where we had a cheerless breakfast and a bottle of light, sparkling wine, which he liked so much that he took the dampened label off and put it in his wallet so that he'd remember it. For the next marriage! She sulked all through and I couldn't very well laugh.

They went to live in the country after the child came and she wrote me a note that I kept. I don't know why I kept it. It said:

Dear Baba,

We are in a valley with a hill of golden, trampled bracken to look out on, and birds are nesting in the hardly-budded trees. We have a grey stone house with stone slates on the roof and wooden beams inside, and white-washed, bumpety walls and pots for flowers everywhere; the boards creak and he loves me and there is something about having a child and being in a valley, and being loved, that is more marvellous than anything you or I ever knew about in our flittery days.

Always, Kate

Always, Kate! I was miserable at the time. Never, Kate! That night I put on my best things and went to an Irish club. Fate of fates I met my builder.

His name was Frank and he was blowing money around the place and telling jokes. I'll repeat one joke so as you'll have an idea how hard up I was – two men with fishing tackle have an arm around an enormous woman and one says to the other, 'A good catch.' When people are drunk they'll laugh at anything, provided they're not arguing, or hitting each other.

Anyhow he drove me home and offered me money – he has a compulsion to offer money to people who are going to say no – and asked if I thought he looked educated. Educated! He was a big, rough fellow with oily hair and his eyebrows met. So I said to him, 'Beware of the one whose eyebrows meet, because in his heart there lies deceit.' And sweet Jesus, next time we met he'd had them plucked over his broken nose. He's so thick he didn't understand that the fact they met was the significant thing. Thick. But nice too. Anybody that vulnerable is nice, at least that's how I feel. Another dinner. Two dinners in one week and a bunch of flowers sent to me. The first thought I had when I saw the flowers was, could I sell them at cut rates. So I offered them to the girls in the bed-sits above and below, and they all said no except one eejit who said yes. She began to fumble for her purse, and I felt so bloody avaricious that I said, 'Here's half of them,' so we had half each and when he came to call for me that evening he counted the number of flowers that I'd stuck into a paint tin, for want of a vase. And you won't believe it, but didn't he go and ring the flower shop to say they'd swindled him. There he was out on the landing phone, yelling into it about how he'd ordered three dozen Armagh roses and what crooks they were, and how they'd lost him as a customer, and there was I in the room with a fist over my mouth to smother the laughing. 'You may not be educated,' said I, 'but you're a merchant at heart. You'll go far.' It ended up by the flower shop saying they'd send more, and they did. I was driven to go out to Woolworths and buy a two-shilling plastic vase because I knew the paint tin would topple if one more flower was put in.

He didn't propose bed for at least six dinners and that shook me. I didn't know whether to be pleased or offended. He was blind drunk the night he said we ought to, and my garret was freezing and far from being a love-nest. The roses had withered but weren't thrown out, and I had this small little bed so that his feet hung out at the bottom. I lay down beside him – not in the bed, just on it – with my clothes on. He fumbled around with my zip and of course broke it, and I thought, I hope he leaves cash for the damage and even if he does I'll have to go to a technical school to learn how to stitch on a zip, it's that complicated. I knew the bed was going to collapse. You always know a faulty bed when you put it to that sort of use. So, he got the zip undone and got past my vest – it was freezing – and got a finger or two on my skin, just around my midriff that was beginning to thicken because of all the big dinners and sauces and things. I reckoned I ought to do the same thing and I explored a bit and got to his skin and the surprising thing was, his skin was soft and not thick like his face. He began to delve deeper, very rapacious at first, and then he dozed off. That went on for a while – him fumbling, then dozing – until finally he said, 'How do we do it?' and I knew that was why he hadn't made passes sooner. An Irishman; good at battles, sieges and massacres. Bad in bed. But I expected that. It made him a hell of a sight nicer than most of the sharks I'd been out with, who expected you to pay for the pictures, raped you in the back seat, came home, ate your baked beans and then wanted some new, experimental kind of sex and no worries from you about might you have a baby, because they liked it natural, without gear. I made him a cup of instant coffee, and when he went to sleep I put a quilt over him and put the light out. I sat on the chair thinking of the eighteen months in London, and all the men I'd met, and the exhaustion of keeping my heels mended and my skin fresh for the Mr Right that was supposed to come along.

I knew that I'd end up with him; he being rich and a slob and the sort of man who would buy you seasick tablets before you travelled. You won't believe it but I felt sort of sorry for him, the way he worried about not being educated, or being fooled by florists, or being taken for an Irish hick by waiters. Never mind that they're Italian hicks. I could tell them all to go to hell because I had a brazen, good-looking face and was afraid of none of them, not even afraid whether people liked me or not, which is what most people are afraid of, anyhow. I know that people liking you or not liking you is an accident and is to do with them and not you. That goes for love too, only more so. Well, to cut a long story short I married him and we had a big wedding with names being yelled out and red carpet to walk on. Strictly speaking it wasn't carpet but cording stuff. Not that I drew his attention to it because he'd have had a fight right there and then with photographers at hand to verify it. We were married by an Abbot from one of the monasteries that Frank's outfit built. The wedding was a big do with speeches about hurling, and happiness, and all sorts of generalized garbage. There were ninety-four telegrams. I learnt afterwards that he had instructed his secretary to send a host of them and put workmen's names to them. He'd die if he didn't get a bigger number of telegrams than anyone else, or make the wittiest speech. It was easy to be witty with the guests we had. He planned his own speech for weeks before. Imagine it. He had a voice trainer come in for four evenings. You'd pay not to talk like her. She was screeching all over the place and he and her were in the room saying 'A' and 'O' for several hours. She was one of those fat Englishwomen that are stuffed with bread, and law-di-daw and nothing else.

Of course everyone got drunk at the wedding and when we got to the aeroplane, me in a powder-blue Paris going-away suit, we couldn't be let on because of him being incapable. He got very obstreperous and said did they know who he was, and did they know his wife was wearing a Balenciaga. Anyhow we had to turn back and the one thing I was relieved about was that he wouldn't want to sleep with me that first night because that was the one thing I dreaded. You see that was the one aspect of him I didn't like at all. I liked his money and his slob ways: I didn't mind holding hands at the pictures but I had no urge to get into bed with him. Quite the opposite.

I even confided in my mother. I hardly ever talked to my mother about anything, because when I was four I had scarlet fever and she sent me away to a Gaeltacht to learn Irish. She really sent me away so that she wouldn't have to mind me – the maid was on two weeks' holiday – but she thought up this Gaeltacht stunt so that it sounded wholesome. I was only there a day when I had to be put in the infirmary. They made me dictate letters, 'Darling Mummy [I'm not your mother, I'm Mummy you used to say], I am getting better, I drank orange juice through a tube this morning. Love to you and Daddy, darling Mummy.'

I don't want to sound all martyrish about it, it's just that I didn't tell her things, but I did mention this physical ordeal and she said it would be all right, to just grit my teeth and suffer it. She said it was because of physical attraction that most marriages went wallop, that physical attraction was another form of dope. Dope was my mother's word for anything that people got by on. I don't hold it against her. I don't expect parents to fit you out with anything other than a birth certificate, and an occasional pair of new shoes. She said what she did, because she was feathering her nest too. That's how he really hooked us – financing us all. Because of his money my mother was over here in London having the life of Riley; her corns attended to, new clothes, gin slings every evening in hotels, and then we'd all (he never stirred with less that ten or twelve people) repair to some joint where a coarse man or woman played the piano and titivated their wares. As if that was exciting. My mother had a right old time. 'He's a good man, your Frank,' she'd say to me across a table in one of those lurid places, and then she'd look around for him and raise her glass and say, 'Frank take care,' and they'd drink to me: the bloody, sacrificial lamb. Twenty years before she wouldn't have let him use the outside lavatory in our house at home. You'll think I'm bitter about my mother but I'm not. She died soon after that. She got cancer of the stomach and died in a matter of months. I believe that for the twenty-four hours before she died she screamed and fought against it and I missed her more than I ever thought I would. I suppose up to the time people die you think their lives will improve, or you'll get on better with them, but once they're dead you know neither thing is possible.

Well, that's how it happened. We moved into a posh house. I love the smell of rich houses, rich shops, flowers and carpets, I'd have the whole world fitted with flowers and carpets if I could. We looked out on the river Thames – great view, storm windows, burglar alarms, double doors, the works. Some of it was a lark, hanging pictures and getting rooms done like the Vatican. Our bathroom was in a fashion magazine with me sitting on my cane throne. We bought dozens of copies and sent them back to Ireland, to the relations. Twin beds for a while until he read that they were out. He got a King-size monstrosity with a Scandinavian head-board. That finished my tranquillity. Apart from anything else he moves in his sleep like a pie-hound, banging and sniffing and rooting all over the place.

Brady came back to London too – nature and silence-in-the-evening didn't work out after all. We met regularly to discuss our plight. Her life like a chapter of the inquisition. He wanted her to stay indoors all the time and nurse his haemorrhoids. One day she had a funny glint in her eye.

'What's up?' said I. I might have known. She'd met someone else, she was in love, the old, old story. She began to rave until I thought I'd puke. He turned out to be prize. They came here in the afternoons for cups of tea, and to talk, I even went out to give them a chance, but they never got past the front room. Songs about the oppressed took over. I used to wonder when it would end, but apart from that I didn't put much consequence on it. Which goes to show how wrong I can be.

2

'Long legs, crooked thighs, small head and no eyes ...'
Her son Cash asked the riddle for the fifth time as they
walked by a gloomy pond, their gloved hands joined.

'A crooked man,' Kate said.

'No. Will I tell you?' the child asked, impatient to air his
knowledge.

'Give me one more chance,' she said and guessed again,
wrongly, 'a crooked woman.'

The child began to laugh aloud in a shrill and forced way.
A thing he did often to try and induce a little gaiety into
their lives.

'A tongs,' he said triumphant, and she bent down and
pressed her damp nose against his. They ought to feed the
ducks so that they could hurry in out of the cold. The pond
was partly frozen, and partly not. Chunks of ice bobbed
about, and the ducks swam around the borders of the ice.
One duck perched on a balcony of ice but got off quickly
finding it so precarious. When they saw the bread they
swarmed towards the bank and the three swans came right
out of the water on to the frozen cinder path. She hated
swans. Their greed. Their ugly bodies. Their webbed, slime-
like feet.

'Mind your glove,' she said. A swan had bitten off the

child's red glove one day, a year before, and carried it to the opposite bank where the park keeper had to rescue it with a hook on the end of a fishing rod.

'Me mind me glove,' the child said.

'Stop talking like a child,' she said as she stood there wondering. How she was going to get away that evening and should she wear her good clothes or not?

It was now between three and four on a winter's afternoon and the light was beginning to fade. It had snowed on and off for several weeks, but because there hadn't been a recent fall what lay on the grass was a soiled and despairing yellow.

'Are you going out tonight?' the child asked. Something momentous about the way he looked up into her face and caught the two tears she had been holding on to, like contact lenses.

'Yes.'

'With Dada?'

'Without Dada.'

'Don't go,' he said, parodying a sad face. He affected sadness as easily as he laughed but that did not mean he wasn't troubled. No more than that her tears were shallow.

'Look,' she said, to distract him, and she held the bag upside-down and sprinkled the remainder of the bread on to the water. The ducks and swans converged on it.

When they got to the waste-paper basket that was nailed to the by-law board she threw the rolled paper bag in, and read for the child's benefit the names of the fish, which according to the notice proliferated in that unlikely half-acre of miserable, stagnant water.

'......, carp, bleak, bream.'

They did not sound like the names of fish at all but like a litany of moods that any woman might feel any Monday morning after she'd hung out her washing and caught a glimpse of a ravishing man going somewhere alone in a motor-car.

No one was out but themselves. It was tea-time and fire-lighting time. The first foul whiffs of smoke rose from several chimneys. She could well believe that there were gas pokers alight in all of these houses. Identical houses with identical things going on behind the brick fronts.

'Do me smell me custard powder?' Cash asked, knowing well that it wasn't. In the summer-time, depending on how the wind blew, they could smell custard powder from some factory. A niceish smell in the light, airy summer days with the electric chime from the ice-cream van, and stoic men sitting on canvas stools fishing for whales in the '.. .. .., carp, bleak, bream' pond. They crossed the road and walked towards their own house.

'That was a short walk,' Eugene said, opening the hall door for them. He had the ashen look that he'd worn through autumn when the light was bronze from the trees outside, and through winter now, his chosen, destined season. Weakness, timidity, guilt overcame her. She thought, 'He knows, he knows. If only he'll give me this last chance, I'll change, reform, make myself so ugly that I will be out of the reach of temptation.'

'The sink smells again. I told you not to strain cabbage or cauliflower down,' he said.

'Maura must have done it. Where is she?' Kate said, relieved that his wrath was for the sink only.

'I don't know where she is,' he said, as Kate advanced towards the well of the stairs and called to the young giggly

12

servant with as much authority as she could muster.

They had steamed fish and cauliflower. The fish had gone cold, and Maura ruined the vegetables by overcooking them.

'All right?' Kate said out of habit. They sat at their accustomed places, he at one end of the mahogany table, she at the other, Cash and Maura in between facing each other, making daft sounds, golluping their food one minute, chewing it to distraction the next minute.

'I wouldn't say it was the best meal I've ever had,' he said, lifting his face from the plate of white, insipid food to stare over her head at the glass-house where the branches of an old vine wormed and gnarled their way.

'Cauliflower needs only a little water,' she said, giving Maura a hint. She wanted to sound practical so that after tea she could decently stand up and say, 'I'm going over to see Baba for a couple of hours.'

Baba, her friend since childhood and now the wedded wife of a builder. Baba owned one ranch mink stole and intended owning several more. She'd even promised one to Kate. Baba had green eyes that drooped at the corners and were inclined to flashes of wickedness. An occasional blow from her husband gave to one or other of those green eyes a permanent knowingness, as if at twenty-five she realized what life was all about. She had plans for them both to leave their husbands one day when they'd accumulated furs and diamonds, just as once she had planned that they would meet and marry rich men and live in houses with bottles of booze opened, and unopened, on silver trays.

As soon as he put the knife and fork down and pushed the plate to the side of the table Kate would tell him that she was going out. Then she would fly upstairs, make her face up, but not overdo it, wear her second-best coat, carry her ear-rings and her fur hat in a paper bag saying it contained home-made scones for Baba, and set out in a flutter. She could put them on, as always, in the Ladies' room of the Underground station.

'I think it's the coldest day we've had,' she said, hoping for a response.

'The wireless says there'll be more snow,' Maura said.

'Oh no,' Kate said, and caught a look from him that said, 'We are all inconvenienced by it, not just little you.'

'Goody, piles and piles of snow, we'll make a snowman.' Cash was always threatening to make a snowman but never did. He hatched indoors like the rest of them. Waiting for the spring.

'You weren't out at all today?' she said to her husband. He wasn't working. He'd saved enough money from the previous project to see them through a few months. He directed documentary pictures but was always buying leisure as if in the course of leisure he most found what he had been ordained to do.

'No,' he said. They were surrounded by silence. Simply to fill in the silence she said that the oil heater in the room tended to give her a headache.

'Oh well, everything has its drawbacks,' he said. Every word pierced. Tonight she would tell her friend that they must not see each other for a while. Anyhow the joy of seeing him was diminishing, and she was more conscious of the risks than of the pleasure. She thought how it is impossible to tell in the beginning of an attraction whether it is the real thing or not.

They'd met at a party and they were attracted to each other the way hundreds of people are, out of hunger. It would have ended there but that they met by accident a few days later, as she was coming out of a white sale.

'Are you plunging in?' she said. There was something cissyish about seeing a man shop for sheets. She had a parcel of them in her hand and a new fur hat on her head. Saved having it wrapped.

'Would you like some tea?' he said, apparently too ashamed to shop now. He steered her down the street to a cramped restaurant with atrocious masks on the wall, and high stools that made no allowance for the small of the back. It was March. Windy. Pieces of paper and dust blowing about, and people with a look of fortitude because they had to fight the wind. He said something about apple blossom, how it was probably blowing about in orchards all over Kent and how he wished he was there. But then he would not have met her! Some such compliment.

He asked her to have tea the following week and she agreed, telling herself that she was not in love with him, and therefore not party to anything wicked. The love came later. Or something bordering on it. They began to meet oftener; they made furtive telephone calls, wrote ardent letters, swore they would have to do something but did nothing. Her husband began to sense it at once, although there was no evidence that he knew. He took to wearing pyjamas in bed, to going for walks alone, to commenting on her slackening midriff. At Christmas, a few weeks before, she gave him a calendar on a marble stand and he said, 'You're sure this is for me?' He produced two packages, one for Cash and one for Maura.

'You forgot me,' she said to him, sullenly.

'I give presents when I want to,' he said, 'not out of duty.'

'You're quite right,' she said, but in the wrong tone.

'I see you're getting your persecution complex back, put a sign out,' he told her, and turned to Cash to explain the principle of the steam train he had just given him. Maura received high boots and matching gloves and she marched round wearing both, hitting her gloved hands together, saying she was well away. It was strange how a happy face automatically became a pretty one.

'You'd like tea or coffee?' Kate said, because he had pushed the half-eaten fish aside and was awaiting the next course. They had no pudding that particular evening.

'Tea.'

She and Maura automatically had the same and Cash had milk, which he drank through a straw to make it exciting. Outside they could hear the spatter of snow falling on the greenhouse. The wind began to howl. For some reason she thought of a dog she'd once known as a child, who had taken fits and had been locked up in an outhouse. She had feared that the dog would break loose and do terrible damage to them, just as now she knew the wind was intending to do harm.

'I hope it's not too bad, I promised Baba I'd go over,' Kate said as casually as her guilt would allow.

'On a night like this?' he said.

'Well I promised,' she said, carrying her own cup of tea out of the room, to the refuge of the freezing upstairs where she adorned her face with vanishing cream and a new gold powder she'd bought.

When she came down she found that he had his coat on and she smiled and asked if he was having a little constitutional.

'I'll come with you,' he said. 'Haven't seen Baba for months.'

'Oh,' she said, getting all solicitous, 'you'd better not, Baba's in trouble. She and Frank are not hitting it off and she wants advice from me.'

'In that case,' he said, 'I'll go somewhere else.'

She almost froze to death. They each kissed the child, warned Maura about the oil heater, and went out into the bitter night.

'Which way are you going?' she said, pausing at the gateway. He did not reply but walked beside her towards a bus stop that was at the end of their road. The steady, pitiless blobs of snow beating against her face, the emptiness and darkness of the street – only two of the seven street lights functioned – irritated. Why could he not use his car like other men? Why did they have to live in that place? she thought, forgetting that she had coaxed him to come there. It was a long, dull street. Trees. Some shed red berries that children later stamped into the tarred road so that they were like the tracks of someone who had gone by bleeding. Deathly quiet in the daytime. Rag-and-bone men rumbling along, yelling an inexplicable cry that she would never have understood except for seeing the junk. And always funerals. Coffins garnished with flowers, one or two courtesy cars following behind. Flowers instead of friends. Death, as bleak as living. She hardly ever talked to her neighbours. No wonder. They were mostly housewives who waved their husbands goodbye in the mornings, shopped around eleven, collected plastic tulips with the packets of dust-blue detergent, and wrote to the County Council about having the trees chopped down. They believed trees caused asthma and were always petitioning her to write and say the same thing.

How did they survive? Endurance! That was a thing to aim at, and maybe asthma. A disease that she could talk about, and use as a weapon to live.

'Missed it!' she said to Eugene as the bus trundled by. They had to wait ten minutes for the next one. She timed it on his watch, touching his wrist each time, to feel his regard for her. Nothing.

The bus had that flat after-Christmas feeling. People with new gloves, handbags, headscarves, were making the dutiful trip to thank whoever had sent them these dull gifts in lovely, frosted-paper wrappings.

'But take me,' a girl behind was explaining. 'People see me and they say, "Hello Judith, how's Janice?"'

'She must be a twin,' Kate said turning to Eugene. He was not listening, his eyes were centred on a beautiful Indian woman who sat quite still, and with such presence that every other woman seemed foolish or strident.

'I should have some Indian children,' he said.

'Cash is all right,' Kate said, prickled.

'Of course he's all right.'

It was useless. He occupied most of the seat too, and was crushing the pleats of her new pleated skirt.

'If you sat on the other seat I'd have more room,' she said to Eugene. The words cut like a lancet through the fog-filled chatter. She stopped short. They looked at each other for some time. It was the last look of pity that passed between them. Each turning to the other had felt the ghost go out. A little phrase had severed them. He moved to the seat behind.

'I was only joking,' she said. He did nothing but smile, a bitter, cunning, tell-you-nothing smile. Kate got out first because Baba's house was near by. She said she'd see him later. The cunning smile ushered her away.

"Bye,' he said.

She crossed the road and took the same number bus back to the station, fretting because she was over an hour late for the appointment with her friend.

3

Kate came into the warm, mahogany-brown pub; looked, and through one of the glass panels she saw him rise to greet her.

'I love you,' he said, even before he said hello. He helped her off with her snowy gloves, so that they could plait fingers in passing.

'Do you hear me?' he asked, his jaw twitching, his top lip yellow from the froth of beer. They moved to the open fire. She caught sight of herself in the old-fashioned overmantel, and saw her nose, not quite purple, but a cold, unlovely blue. The gold powder was a sell.

'Look,' he said, as if it were their last chance of saying anything, 'I thought how ghastly if you didn't come.'

'Well I did,' she winked to seem funny for him. Mad. Mad.

They sat themselves on a long stool behind a stained, unsteady table, spreading out their coats and their drinks to discourage others from sitting next to them. He had a large whisky waiting for her, and beer and whisky for himself which he drank from alternate glasses.

'I would never do it like that,' she said and looked away knowing she was going to do it another way. She knew his face by heart anyhow: a pleasant, full face that was not over-full, blue, affectionate eyes, one jaw that twitched, waved greying hair and a ring on his marriage finger. That irked.

'Tell me everything, what you've been doing and thinking', and then he said quickly, 'I have so much to tell you.'

Would he leave his wife, forfeit his chance in politics? Sometimes he was reckless but only in drink. He was drunk now. They could go on exactly as they were. But no, they'd already worn it out, with talk.

'I couldn't be without you – it would be like dying,' she said. A sentence that he'd nursed when she first spoke it months ago. She thought that phrases were like melodies, they went on appealing long after one had stopped listening. Then one day they fell out of favour.

'I am alive, and in some ways happy,' he said. His bloodshot eyes closed on her face many times, either because they were tired, or because he wanted to feast on the image of her.

'I am not,' she said, without humour.

'I would bless you for that,' he said.

'Why?'

'Because you are candid, honest, outright.'

He ought to be prime minister; he had a fierce gift for words.

'Really?' she said, believing and not believing him.

'That is the truth of it,' he said.

It was quiet except for the soft hiss of soda being splashed from a siphon down the side of a glass. She looked around to search the faces near to her to see if there was anyone listening.

'I hate to say it,' she began, 'but everything at home is getting worse, bleak.' It was not so much that she hated to say it, as that she was inadequate. How could she give any notion of what it was like to ascend her own stairs, meet her own husband on the first landing, see him turn away and hear him cough politely as if she were a deformed person? Anyhow, it was not for this kind of chat that her friend picked her that windy far-off day.

'Dear God,' he said, beating his forehead, 'I am now filled with blackness.'

'Forgive me,' she said.

'Of course,' he said. 'I knew it anyhow. We are as one, I knew it by your face.'

'I look awful,' she said, seeking flattery.

'On the contrary. How very beautiful you are, your face has a new dimension.'

He was overdoing it again. He ordered large drinks, they clenched hands, sat like two people in an air-raid shelter wondering why they had come down there and not met death up above.

'We are guilty,' he said, 'and no doubt. But who is to judge us? It happened.'

'It happened,' she repeated after him, as if they were on trial.

'What will we do?' she said. He beat his lined forehead again, curled and uncurled his square-tipped fingers, searched for her hand, swore at the gods, and called her 'Milis', which is the Gaelic for sweet.

'The world is hard,' he said at last. She did not doubt it, he had a leaden wife and school bills for five children, and a town house and a country house and a job to keep. At least she could mope around all day and dwell on her unhappiness, but he had to work; keep his minister informed of things, appease the voters, ward off complainers, dress well, and make conversation at ludicrous dinner parties engineered for reasons quite separate from friendship. He had to pretend to cope.

'So what ought we do?' she said.

'No harm must be done, to anyone,' he said.

'It has been done,' she said, not knowing the full truth and consequence of her remark.

Then he said what she expected of him, and almost what she wished: that they must not meet for a while, that they must suffer it, that they must consider the feelings of other people, that they must cling to the seeds of their love and spit out the unpleasant but necessary pips. More apple images. She nodded, and shivered, and half-wept, and drank, and re-shivered. She thought of a girl she knew who wrote a letter to a man and finding that it was not soulful enough she sprinkled it with tap-water to convince him more.

'You know what I know,' he said, holding both her hands in both of his, 'and how I care.' She returned from the trance of his strong, preaching, Welsh accent stating their respective duties, returned to the noise and fog-laden smoki-ness within the pub. And felt a little fortified. It was almost closing time. Meanwhile, the place had filled up and Irish barmen were going around collecting glasses, and yelling at the late comers who circled the brown, solid counter, jostling for service.

'Let's go,' he said. Out in the street, because it was late and in a minute many more people would clamour for taxis, they took the one that came instantly. He kissed her a troubled good night. He was already three hours late for his dolorous wife.

'Sit on it, lock it up, be brave,' he said as she vanished inside, and deposited herself on the cold, leather seat and heard him ask what the fare would be. He had nice ways.

She thought of asking the driver to let her out so that she could telephone Baba and make sure her lie had gone unquestioned. But it was late and she had no coins, and anyhow since the affair had terminated her guilt and unease seemed to lessen. They merely deluded themselves about postponing it; it was over.

It was a mean thought and she knew that but she still wished that she had asked him to return the skeleton of the leaf. Probably he had lost it or left it between the pages of a long-winded report. She suddenly attached superstition to it, its return would preface the return of everything good. It had been a gift from her husband, this skeleton leaf, mouse-brown in colour with a fine lace texture and a tail long and thin like a mouse too. A delicate thing created by chance in the autumn when it fell and the flesh of the leaf shrivelled away. They got it in Wales. She gave it to her friend the third time they met and now she wanted it back.

She was like that, she gave too quickly. She did not have her husband's instinct to preserve. She thought of him throughout the drive. Not as he was at dinner but as she remembered him before. Calling her out of a crowded room once, simply to kiss her, and go back in again. And she had prayed into his mauve tongue that such a miracle would last for ever. Prayed one thing and done another. Tonight she was returning to him. She would communicate it in some way, linger over him, pour myrrh on his scalded soul, ask him to forget, forget and forgive, the way the song said.

'Here, just here,' she said. The taxi had gone several doors past her house. Just as well. She got out and walked back, planning how she would break the ice with him. The snow was thick and vaporous in the pathway and the tracks of his twelve-inch, crêpe-soled shoes were fresh on it.

4

Kate came in quietly and found him in the study standing over Maura who was sitting on the couch. At first it seemed as if he had his arms around the girl.

'Oh togetherness,' Kate said. 'Perhaps I'm too early.' He turned round, acknowledged the fact that he saw her and returned to attend to Maura's eyes. He was obviously taking out a smut because he had a small paint-brush in one hand, and an eye-glass fixed in the socket of his left eye.

'It's all right, sir, it's all right,' Maura said, as she leapt up and went out of the room.

'Well, that's one way of returning,' Eugene said.

'Have I done something wrong?' she said gently, undoing the last two buttons of her coat.

'No, no, just your customary kindness,' he said.

'Oh,' she said and waited. She would have to withdraw the remark.

'I think if you make too free they take advantage,' she heard herself say.

'Indubitably.' A word he used when he had no intention of saying anything.

'She drinks milk straight from the bottle, it's rimmed with lipstick.' She, who meant to dispense only kindness.

'Baba's well,' she said then, in the hope of retrieving the

evening. She had her coat across her arm and was intending to hang it near the fire in a moment.

'Cheers,' he said. 'I was breathless to hear how she was.' She stood wondering, then asked if she could get him some supper, and when he declined she asked why in a grieved tone. He didn't feel like supper. He felt like tidying all his records, dusting the sleeves, putting some sort of order into them.

'I thought of making soup for us.' She stood there at a loss, chagrined, sorry, moving from one foot to the other, thinking that as she counted ten he would say something to detain her. He was in one of his moods. He reminded her then of a lightning conductor, tuned only to the elements, indifferent to people. His back was getting thicker or perhaps it was the winter woollens that made him shapeless. He still held himself more erect than anyone she knew.

'Well, I suppose I'd better go to bed,' she said.

'Suppose you'd better.' He did not turn round and give the semblance of a kiss by making a kiss-noise, as was his habit lately.

Upstairs she lay awake and planned a new, heroic role for herself. She would expiate all by sinking into domesticity. She would buy buttons, and spools of thread other than just black and white; she would scrape marrow from the bone and mix it with savoury Marmite to put on their bread; she would put her lily hand down into sewerages and save him the trouble of lifting up the ooze, and hairs, and grey slime that resulted from their daily lives. She listened in vain for sounds.

When she came down in the morning she looked for clues to his humour. There was the skin of an apple on a plate, and the daily sentence in block capitals for Cash to write out. Until such time as he went to school his father wrote something out for him to copy. Underneath there was a scribbled sentence, which Kate took to be a memento for herself:

Now and then he thought all women could not possibly be bitches, but not for long, reality was always at hand.

She read it a few times but decided not to comment on it.

At twelve o'clock as usual, she brought his tea on a tray, but she chose a nicer cloth, and had worried away the tea-stains in his china cup by applying bread soda.

'I thought I'd do it properly,' she said, as he sat up and reached out for the heavy, thick-knit jersey on the floor.

'Yes,' he said, 'it helps to make an effort.' She sat on the side of the bed, holding the tray that he had balanced perfectly on his knees. He kept looking at one pane of the diamond-paned window. It was caked with snow.

'I must clean those windows,' she said, trying to humour him. She both knew and did not know that what she said had come too late. Finally, when she'd made no progress, she went downstairs calling Cash. He was with Maura, dancing to pop music from the radio. Like a little miniature man he steered the clumsy, pink-armed girl around, and smiled lovingly up into her jolly, flushed face.

'It's time we got on with the lunch,' Kate said in a pinched voice.

'Oh no,' the child said, 'me like dancing.' His mother put her arms out and drew him from the warm kitchen into another room, where she reclaimed him with frantic kisses.

'What game will we play?' she said, humouring him.

'Put treasure in a box,' he said, 'and draw a map and I'll look for it.'

She found a box under a sofa where Eugene stuffed things – papers, maps, books, shoe-trees, carrier bags, fishing rods.

'What will we put in it?' she asked.

'Treasure.'

'Sixpence?'

'No.'

'What?'

'I *told* you. Treasure.'

From upstairs she heard Eugene call, 'Turn off that cat-alley moaning.'

Maura still had the radio going, full blast.

'Turn off that cat-alley moaning,' Kate said, passing on the blame.

She put a bead from a broken necklace in the box, drew the map and sat there while her son crawled around the room asking if he was getting hot or cold, depending on where he was. She said what she had to say, but had no heart in it.

For weeks Eugene barely spoke. It continued to snow. Bulky icicles hung from the ledge of the coal bunker and when they washed clothes they had to dry them indoors. The quiet, sad drip of the wet clothes and his silence were the only sounds she heard during those weeks. He put ammonia around the house in saucers to take the sulphur fumes away, and when the fog came down in the evening it too seemed not to move nor wander the way fog does, but to stand still and be hardened by the frost. Even the clothes stiffened in the night, if the boiler went out.

He's freezing me out, she thought as she watched for him to get up, to eat his toast, to go to the lavatory, to put on his coat, to go out, and then hours later to come back in again. Sometimes, if there was a programme in his pocket, she knew he'd been to a concert or to a theatre. Jealousy drove her to search for ticket stubs, to see if there were one or two, but he was careful not to leave anything like that around. She hardly slept, except for the first half-hour after getting into bed, when she would fall asleep from total exhaustion and then waken crying, fully alert to everything. They shared the same bed, but he saw to it not to retire until it was morning and time for her to get up.

Once, she stayed on in the morning, and in his sleep, he touched her and drew back suddenly, as if he were an animal who had just touched an electric fence and received an appalling shock. For the first time she looked old, really old.

5

One day after lunch Kate took several swigs of whisky from a bottle that she kept in her handbag, and braved it.

'What are we doing, what are we doing?' she said to Eugene, thinking that by an open appeal she would break through to him.

'I haven't noticed that I struck you lately.' He was putting his coat on to go out.

'We're like enemies. We're not like man and wife at all.'

'I should hope not.'

'But why?' she begged. 'Why? Why?' After all, he had been the one to urge marriage and child on her, and he must have known that she was incontinent.

'It's not just my fault, it's yours too, it's ours,' she said, thinking guiltily of all the women's things he had done for the child, like putting a drawstring of twine through a Fair-Isle jersey that did not gather in around the neck.

'I must say it took me quite a time to get to know you,' he said. 'I must congratulate you on your simpleton's cunning, and your simpleton's servile ways.'

He, who exacted obedience!

'We all have faults,' she said, moving back a bit in case he smelt the whisky and delivered a lecture about alcohol.

'Fortunately some of us know about honour,' he said. It was strange, though consistent, how in a row he stiffened and talked the wooden language of tracts.

'Honour,' she said, unable to think of her own words or resort to her own argument.

'The things you do, count, not your cheap little justifications.' He had his grey flannel scarf on and was smoothing his hair down before putting a corduroy cap on. Luckily Maura and Cash were out feeding the ducks so they could talk without fear of being heard.

'Can't we talk,' she said, 'really talk?' Even if they did what would they say? He had been a great believer in airing one's difficulties, but at this point neither of them was capable of listening.

He was giving his attention to the cap.

'Eugene,' she said desperately.

He moved his face from its image in the mirror and looked at her, as though looking at the most ultimate outrage that could have befallen him. Where was the woman he had never had the good fortune to meet?

'We'll get over it, we'll get through it,' she said, pitying him, pitying herself. 'I'll be better.'

He shook his head and looked at her grimly, the look of a gravedigger.

'You don't. It's your nature to lie like your lying, lackeying ancestors.'

'Oh stop,' she said, gripping him.

'Excuse me, I detest vulgarity,' he said, picking her arm up and dropping it at her side. He put his hand on the door catch.

'Just say one nice thing,' she said, trembling. If he went now it was final. Because his temperament − at least he called it temperament – was so, that when people failed him he detached himself from them completely. They ceased to exist any more for him.

'You live your life, I live mine. That's fair, isn't it?' He had opened the door and icy air rushed into the hall.

'Where will I live?'

'Plenty of cosy bed-sitting rooms around.'

Was he telling her to go?

'And Cash?' she said.

'I might let you see him on humanitarian grounds, but of course your morals make you unfit to be a mother.' The two words 'humanitarian' and 'morals' stuck out like barbs on wire. And the tears she shed now were tears of rage and self-pity.

'I didn't sleep with him,' she said. It was no longer necessary to hide about Duncan. She wished she had the courage to say the word fuck and offend him more.

'The intention was there,' he said. 'In the eyes of the law that is what counts.'

'You bastard,' she said directly to his grey-flannel face. In his mind he had already dealt with her and meted out the punishment that a judge would have done.

'You vicious bastard,' she said.

He struck her once across the cheek.

'That's right, hit me,' she said. 'Contradict all your noble, potty theories.' He believed in the gentle art of persuasion, in change through knowledge, in the twentieth-century game of brain washing. One cheek blazed while the other felt as cold as stone.

'I don't have to,' he said, almost smiling. 'There are other things I can do.' And he went out.

'But what things?' she called, but the men shovelling

snow off the footpath made it impossible for her to repeat it. She was in her bedroom slippers and could not very well follow him out. She ran to the window and watched him walk down the street, his gait free as a man who had just had lunch and was enjoying a little fresh air. True, what he once said to her about being born to stand outside windows and look in at the lit-up muddle of other people's lives. The scene they had just had was *her* scene, not *theirs*. He was apart from it; as he said in jest, he did not attach himself to living people. To sky, to stones, to young girls, he said. To young girls, she thought bitterly, whom he would never meet and therefore never know well enough to despise.

She went upstairs to find the handbag with the broken clasp in which she'd hidden Duncan's love letters. Better put them in the boiler before things became terrible. The bag was wrapped in the nightdress – the very one in fact that she wore when the water broke and Cash was pushing his way into the world – just as she'd left it. She pulled it open and found that the letters were gone. The inside of the bag, smeared with face powder, was treacherously empty. A small typed note fell out:

They are where you cannot find them, safe with my lawyer. I have no doubt but that they will come in useful.

She trembled with shame, with anger that he should know and not have confronted her, that he should have confiscated them and not be ashamed, that he should be as small and mean and obsessional as herself.

She ran downstairs, opening drawers and books, wildly

and without direction. She opened a ledger in which he normally kept notes about his earnings, his health and the weather, and on the centre page she found her obituary:

So this is her, my special, hand-picked little false heart, into whose diseased stinking mind, and other parts, I have poured all that I know about living, being and loving. Tonight I had the pleasure of actually seeing her in the arms of that chinless simpleton whom we met months ago at D.'s party. At supper she patently lied to me about having to see Baba and I accompanied her, guessing that her excuses were flimsy. She could not bring me to Baba, it was too private, she got off a bus, took another, donned some idiotic clothes in a Ladies' room and went to a pub to be with him. I could have gone in and knocked out the few front teeth he has left but it would have been contamination. I went to a pub down the street and had a whisky and got home in plenty of time to await her. I did not tackle her. There is no need to now. In a way it is a relief to know it is over. Somehow I always knew she would destroy it.

It was dated correctly. He'd written it the night she saw Duncan last. He'd even blotted it carefully, not one smear, and commas in the right places.

For the first time she felt some intimation of the enormity of his buried hatred for her, for women, for human follies. There was no doubt about what she must do. She sought out Cash and Maura, sent the girl on a half-day and brought Cash home, telling him they were going on a little journey. She packed some things into a suitcase and some boxes, and prayed that they would get away without being caught. She'd rung Baba and a taxi was on its way to take them from the violated lair to somewhere less awful.

6

S he came here later in a taxi carrying two fibre suitcases and two cardboard boxes. Stuff that I wouldn't be seen dead with.

'Are we on our holidays?' the kid kept saying because of the luggage. Not that it looked jolly. Far from it.

'Come in,' I said. Because I knew everything she was going to say before she said it.

'Oh, Baba,' she said, 'I think I'm going to kill myself.'

'Come on, girl,' I said, 'facts.'

'He found out about Duncan,' she said. 'He hit me and threatened to take Cash away and he hates me.' Millions of women getting hit every day, and I myself forced to strip once on the imprimatur of my husband because three of his pals bet I had no navel. How could I have functioned without a navel? The telephone rang.

'Don't answer it,' she said, jumping up. She said he'd be on her trail soon. He was out for a walk and would come in and find her note.

'What's in the note?' I asked.

'Just that we weren't right for each other.'

Imagine leaving a note like that when he was a fanatical man.

'He says I'm rotten,' she said. He was full of character of

course and she wasn't. She wasn't bad, but like any woman she'd take mission money to buy clothes, or if she met some man she liked she'd persecute him until she had loaded him with the love trophy. Knowing this about her, Eugene was so righteous he made a constant splash about his integrity. They were mad in two different ways.

'I've left,' she said. 'It's all over.' She'd obviously done some very thorough packing because the kid was unloading the contents of the boxes into our elegantly louvred drawers: curtain rings, empty perfume bottles, old envelopes, broken belts.

'What you bring that junk for?' I said.

'Association,' she said, without a smile.

Association or not she'd have to take them away. Frank wouldn't have her in our house with danger brewing. Frank was very careful; you know, slaughter your wife so long as you do it indoors.

'Who's that?' the child said, holding two photographs. One of Kate as a kid leaning on her mother's shoulder. It was the mercy of God her mother got drowned or she'd still be going around tacked on to her mother's navel. And one of Eugene looking like an advertisement for hemlock. That, as you can imagine, started her off on a right orgy of drip. His strong face. Where had it gone wrong? A year ago she had written evidence from him that she was the genuine Kate in ten thousand Kates, because of her alarmingly beautiful face, and disposition, her tender solicitude and worth; and she'd written back to him – he was only in the other room, for God's sake – that he was her buoy, her teacher, the good god from whose emanations she gained all.

'Ring Duncan,' I said. I would have said, 'Ring the Prime Minister' if I'd thought it would have helped. I sent her upstairs to do it in privacy while I chatted up the kid. It was really serious for me. She didn't know it, but Frank got very difficult after we were married. He stopped being a slob, if you know what I mean. I traced all back to the evening of our wedding. For a start we were refused admission on the plane because of his being drunk and he said did they know that his wife was wearing a Balenciaga while they hauled him away to cool off in some private room. Next day when we got away – to some bloody resort that an agent fixed for us – there were gangs of men smirking at me in my buff-coloured suit, and he sent me upstairs to put something respectable on. I owned nothing respectable. At dinner he said the food was oily. He's the sort who, the minute he gets across the English Channel, says the food is oily. That night to add to our joys I had the curse – excitement or some bastard thing – even though I'd worked out all my dates well ahead. He wanted to call a doctor.

'What curse?' he kept saying, as if I was a witch or something.

'It must be the food,' he said. He'd pushed the twin beds together and everything.

'Don't you know about women?' I said. He just looked at me with his big, stupid, wide-open mouth. He didn't know. What sort of mother had he? He said to leave his mother out of it, that she was a good woman and baked the best bread in Ireland. I said there was more to life than baking good bread. He got vicious then. And went down to the bar. The upshot was that we didn't sleep together that night and when we did a few nights later it was pretty uneventful. For me that is. He said what was wrong with me. I said it wasn't as simple as he thought, that for women hand manipulation, coaxing, et cetera had to come into it. He said I made us sound like a bleeding motor engine. But as I saw it he was the one who treated us as an engine. If things go wrong at the start they often stay wrong. He knew no other way and neither did I. Birds of a feather ... As time went on he minded that I wasn't getting preg. – interceding to the Holy Spirit we were – and he'd say to me in front of people, 'Baba, you'll have to go to a doctor and have yourself seen to.' And then, in a drunker state he'd look at some little man who was father of five and say, 'I'm not half the man you are.' I don't know what was up with him. I could never figure out whether it was his mother, or indoctrination from one of those flogging Christian brothers, or had he been with sheep and chickens as a kid and got all his associations, as Kate would put it, mixed up. It changed him though. He got very rough in his ways and would say 'Cut it out' if I said he ought to see a doctor and discuss seeds. He took a great interest in crime and murder and filed the really juicy ones. I could see that bull-fighting would be tops on the agenda.

'I'll ask thee a riddle,' said Cash, looking into my face. He says 'thee' to get attention. I must have been miles away.

'Long legs, crooked thighs, small head and no eyes?' he said. I'm supposed to be as surprised as hell. He's a pure slob really because I taught him that riddle, and he expected me to be dope enough not to know it. I answered wrong. I suppose I liked him. I could see that his father would go mad to lose him. Anyone would. His mother came in just as he was telling me the answer.

'A tongs,' he was saying, his front teeth square and very white, but one chipped at the edge.

'No one is sincere.' She was wringing her hands.

'He's coming on a white horse,' I said, knowing the worst.

She shook her head and repeated the conversation to me, verbatim. It went more or less like this:

'Did he ring you?' she said to her Duncan.

'No, should he?'

'I've just left him; it was awful.'

'That's terrible, Kate.'

'He'll be ringing you, Duncan. He found your letters and everything.'

'Good God, I wouldn't have wished that.'

'Well, it's happened now. He's furious.'

'I wouldn't wish him an hour's, nay, a second's unhappiness.'

'Duncan, will you help me? I'm desperate.'

'But of course. You must think first of him, after all it is between him and you. Go back, talk it over, iron it out.'

That more or less concluded it. He begged her to ring him next morning, but we knew that he'd have some hatchet-voiced secretary laid on to tell Kate some boring and familiar lie, like that he was in conference.

'Time is running out,' she said, looking straight at the grandfather-clock. Talk about being worried. I was a wreck myself, with Frank due any minute.

'Premises,' I said. 'We'll have to get you some.' I knew of a sanitary shop on the King's Road where they leave the baths out all night and I said she could rip up there, sleep in a bath, and put a sign up: 'Keep out. Gonorrhoea.' She'd be safe, like a titless woman. Do you think she'd laugh? Not a glimmer.

'I could book you in a hotel,' I said. I hated to say, 'You can't stay here.'

'I'm in your way. I'm a nuisance,' she said. Damn right, she was. I'm a pure phoney – I heard myself say,

'No, but eventually you'd like a place of your own.'

'Yes,' she said, 'I'd like a studio with white walls and pictures, and a garden smothered in hedge.'

I thought if she goes on like that I won't have to worry, there'll be a team of doctors in here to certify her.

'But for tonight,' I said, 'I'll get you both a hotel.'

'No,' she said, clinging to me, 'we can't go out, he'll take Cash. We must stay here, we must.'

'Me like it here,' the kid was saying like a skilled black-mailer. He was flicking through our leather-bound encyclopedia – nothing, Frank says, like a self-educated man – having demolished a tin of cocktail snacks.

'Now don't worry. Leave it to me,' I said, calming her down. Madman, I am.

The bloody phone rang again.

'Hello, Eug,' I said to stop him in his tracks. Lucky it wasn't him, because of course I gave us away rightly. It was Frank to say he'd met a bunch of very interesting people, and I was to get my Dior on, and come on, because he was taking us all to a new restaurant.

'Super, darling,' I said. That must have shook him, because since the argument over my navel I haven't associated with his mates.

'When and where?' I said. At least 'twould keep him out of the house till late, and Brady could hide until morning. I wrote down the details and told him to take care, which was strange coming from me. Normally I'm praying he'll fall off a scaffold.

She made me go round the house with a crow-bar closing all the windows. She said she didn't think she'd live the night and even the kid was beginning to fret.

'Listen, listen,' she'd say every time a board creaked or

42

the boiler let out some sort of noise. It was like being at a suspense picture only worse. Plenty of human interest! Was I glad to go out! We made an arrangement that I'd telephone once, put the telephone down and then dial again immediately. Otherwise she was to answer nothing. I conducted her to a room at the top of the house where Frank kept easels and things since the time he had the urge to be a painter.

'I wouldn't wish you an hour's, nay, a second's unhappiness,' I said, trying to be funny, as I put a pile of blankets, sheets and pillows into her arms. She looked about eighty, and the kid had his face to the wall sniffling. Had she landed us in a mess!

'I'm meeting men – I'll get you fixed up with one,' I said. She put on the droopy, look-upon-me-with-pity face. But boy did she destine our future!

I got there in my gold shoes and the Dior dress with the enormous rosette on the back. It transpired that he'd met an actor that day – nearly ran over him in the street – and they got chatting and the actor introduced him to a poet, and the poet to a drummer, and the drummer to a Jew, and they had all foregathered for grub. The locals in the pub nudged themselves when I took off my coat. Because of the place the rose was positioned.

'Meet my wife, my wife,' Frank kept saying.

There were two other women in the party: a blonde with the roots badly done and a very quiet-spoken American girl. The actor had just come from work and Frank was fussing over him and buying quadruple brandies. It was the first actor he ever met, for God's sake.

'He's a good actor, keep him happy, keep him entertained,' Frank kept saying to me.

In my experience actors have a hernia if anyone else does the entertaining. I sang dumb except to say 'Chin-chin' at each round.

'I must congratulate you on your taste,' he said to Frank, meaning that I was dishy. I thought it a bit of a neck, but I let it go because I was trying to edge my way across to talk to some real men. The Jew looked interesting and sort of wronged, so did a small pale boy – you couldn't call him a man even though he was about twenty-five or -six – with a girlish face. Dead wrong for a man of course, but still ... His complexion was blue as if he'd been left out nights when he was young, and his lips had no colour, and his hands were about as big as a child's. I never got near him because Frank said the actor was hungry and the muses must be fed. You know that sort of faker-than-fake talk. Before leaving he stuffed pound notes into a couple of collection boxes that were on the counter.

'Poor hungry devils,' he said, meaning neglected dogs or kids or whatever he was financing. Charity! He and the brother sack men on Christmas Eve and re-hire them on St Stephen's day to escape holiday pay. He dropped about ten quid in all.

The restaurant was so new that there was no one else there except us. That sort of shook Frank but the poet said we'd make it swing, so we began to troop around and pretend we were about two hundred people. The pale boy drummed on the table-cloth. I reckoned he was the drummer.

'Sit, lads, sit,' Frank said, the old accent getting bog-thick with drink and excitement.

The place itself was very posh with built-in sand dunes and cacti and water sprays. Like a bloody jungle if you want to know. I could see Frank taking stock of it all. For our interior decor. We were in our rented-flower era. A firm sent a man around every Monday morning to take away a big, vulgar display of plastic flowers and replace it with another. Identical. I suppose they swapped them around from house to house. He was planning to hire a dance floor too, since the day he saw a van go by which said 'Hire your own dance floor and be smart'.

'Are they lilies?' he said, looking at some chrysanthemums.

'Quite,' said the actor. An ignoramus too.

'Give me wax roses any old time,' I said. I was dead drunk, mainly from nerves.

'Do you like gardening?' the actor said to me. God Almighty, what grouping! I was beside him again.

'When I was in the convent,' said I – when tight I get reminiscent – 'we had to till a patch of garden – life is a garden, old chap – and I used to steal flowers from other girls' plots and stick them in my own. I didn't even plant *them* properly!'

Damn actor didn't wait to hear the end of the story.

'Let's have some of the old Mateus, "Amigo",' he was saying to Frank, coming it all Continental. You know, greengrocer's son from Wakeley with his eye on a knighthood.

'What play are you in?' said I. I knew if 'twas posh we'd have heard.

'Is it Shakespeare?' said Frank. He knows about nothing else.

'Actually,' said the actor, and then started up a fit of coughing and stammering and took five minutes to tell us he was in a thing called 'Something, Something, Rubbish'. At that minute the poet cocked his ear. 'Oh,' said the poet, who'd timed it beautifully, the way spiteful people do, 'he is the hind legs of a good old British horse.'

'I'm the front legs,' said the actor, going all blubbery. 'You are a very naughty blond Christopher.' I knew by the way the one smirked, and the other sulked, that they lived together and that the American girl was wasting her bosoms raving away to the poet about iambic pentameter, when she'd be better off at home in Minnesota having dull old fun. They were ill matched: the actor was long and thin with a sort of 'hold-my-hand-Mammy' expression, and the poet was wiry with a hard, hungry, jaundiced face. For some reason, I thought of Kate wringing her boring hands out, and it occurred to me that they might have her as a lodger. I knew that queers like to have a woman around for status so long as they don't have to lay a finger on her, and boy was she straight out of some chastity unit.

'What are we all having?' the actor said. He stuttered ever so nicely. I expect he went to that school where you are thought sensitive if you stutter.

'I don't know,' I said. The menu was like the Magna Carta.

'We'll have soup, lads,' Frank said. I tried to catch his eye to get him off the soup jazz. He thinks it's the poshest thing out. He *knows* it isn't, but he thinks it is, because they only had it once or twice when he was a kid. I made a face at him.

'Stop worrying how much it's going to cost,' said he to me, real loud. That's what I mean about him getting treacherous.

In the end we ordered oysters and snails and swank stuff. While the food was coming someone said that someone ought to tell a joke.

'Yes, sport,' said the Australian. I forgot to say there was an Australian among us and every time he opened his mouth it was to tell some dirty story and the actor would intervene and say, 'Ladies present.' Pure routine jokes about bishops and dirty postcards.

'You should see your face,' said the drummer, leaning across the table to me. I knew I looked bored. He said he liked my story about the flower garden. He said it was anarchy and he liked anarchy.

'Plenty more where that came from,' I said. He was giving me the eye all right. It was ages since I'd had a fling.

'Don't look so furious,' he said. It was then I missed the Jew. He'd quietly left us.

'You don't know anybody who has a studio to let?' I said, leaning too, to meet the drummer half-way across the table. We both had our elbows up shutting out the others. I didn't go on about the white walls and privet hedge bit in case he thought I was nuts.

'I may do,' he said. He had a low conniving voice. Dead sexy.

The waiter was putting down plates of snails and various consignments of cutlery and Frank was telling everyone not to give a minute's thought to the cost, while we all decided on steak and celery. You know how it is in a big restaurant, one person says steak and they all say steak. The blind leading the blind. The head waiter was pressing us to have the plate of the day but we were wise to that. No chicken gizzards for us. He looked mummified. Before that Frank had to bribe him with a fiver to admit the poet, in a boiler suit. As far as I'm concerned it's much more ridiculous to be bribing waiters than to own a presentable suit, but you know the length some people will go to, to be thought rebellious.

'A studio for yourself?' the drummer said to me, real

interested. I suppose I looked rich with my Dior and my rings and gear.

'For a friend,' said I, hoping Frank wouldn't hear. I knew I should ring Kate but kept postponing it.

'We'll talk about it,' said the drummer, while Frank lifted the booze out of the ice-bucket and drenched the hands of the two who were next to him.

'How marvellous,' said the American girl. We were getting the actor's account of how he lived on kippers for three years when he toured the provinces. I know that story backwards. If it was true of even five per cent of the people who tell it there wouldn't be one kipper left in the world. The poet rounded it off with some corny verse and Frank started to clap.

'How did you get to be a poet?' said he real awed. 'Did you enter for a competition?'

Well of course everyone began to laugh and Frank didn't know why.

'I would have thought it started that way,' said he, making a bigger fool of himself.

'Your approach if I may say so is distinctly amateur,' said the poet and Frank knew there was an insult there. He got flushed the way he does before he starts a fight. God, I thought, the lilies and furniture and stuff are in for a bit of reorientation now when he wrecks the joint. I didn't care because the drummer and I were playing what the actor would call 'footsie' under the table, and having a rare time. He began it. I felt this thing on my leg and I thought it was a mouse and nearly screamed, but he stopped me with a look. I have this daft thing about mice. See them out of the corner of my eye when they're not there. Pure lunacy but I do. It was his toe. I wouldn't let him go too far of course. I knew that tune about being hard to get et cetera. We were both chewing away like fiends and didn't as much as look at each other. The old chairs were creaking under us, but no one heard because the actor was trying to get Frank and the poet to shake on it and be friends. Boy, was he a coward.

'Yes,' the American girl was saying to my drummer, 'I'm all right now, I've got the world by the short hairs.' He was smiling away and she thought it was for her, but I could see the little flush in his cheeks.

'That's why I can never ignore it,' the actor said to me, all of a sudden.

'What?' said I, thinking he had gauged the proceedings.

'The telephone,' said he. 'My dear old mother is alive, she lives on solvents now, she is likely to die any minute.'

That sort of brought me back to life, that and his asking me what pudding I would like. There are people in the world and you know they are going to say pudding, and tell you about their mothers living on solvents.

'No pudding,' said I, sort of flat and lonesome now, because I'd dismissed the old toe before things got too runny.

'I'm altering,' said the actor, and I thought why does he have to get confidential with me over dinner, but in fact he was telling the waiter that he'd have a choc ice instead of vanilla.

'I'm serious about this studio,' I said to the drummer.

He looked sort of huffed now as if he mightn't go on with it.

The rest of the evening was uneventful, except that Frank fell asleep before the coffee came and they all nearly died of shock in case they'd have to pay. They got him awake with shaking him and boy did the poet hand out a lot of baloney about the best way to make friends with a good man was to have a row with him.

It worked out easy for me to give the drummer a lift in my Jag because Frank was taking the others in his. That American girl came too. She kept calling the drummer Harvey all the time. We dropped her and then went on to his place.

'Do you want to see the studio?' he said when we got there. We'd been talking real cool in the car.

We went up some flights of stairs – me holding on to the shaky railing – and the linoleum gave out after the third flight. I thought of Brady making a big song and dance about this, saying how environment affects the mind and so forth.

'It's your studio,' I said as we went in, and he switched on a lamp, showing the big room, a tossed bed, a chest of drawers with no handles, two drums and coloured pictures of nudes pinned to the wall.

'Why is it to let?' I said. 'Are you leaving?' We were dead formal, like house agent and client.

'Yes,' he said, 'I don't fancy it. It's too bourgeois for me!' Bourgeois. There were orange boxes as chairs, for God's sake, and a floor mat over the bed.

'It's for a friend, a girl, who's left her husband,' I said, in case he thought I wanted it for a love-nest.

'It's not for you,' he said, smiling. He had this fab smile.

'Not me. I live with my husband.'

'Will he expect you home?'

'Sure.'

'In that case,' he said, 'let's be practical. We can't tonight, so why waste time and make him suspicious. When can I come?'

Talk about alacrity. I fixed it that he come to tea next day and then I had a quick look around to see if Brady would find the place habitable. There wasn't a cup or saucer, or any evidence of eating.

Just before I left he put the light out. 'Open your mouth,' he said and gave me this kiss. I went down the rickety stairs singing 'Careless Love' to my heart's content.

I got home in about ten minutes and walked straight into tallyhoo. Old Eugene was there acting like a madman. You know, talking about the law and civil rights and stuff. At four in the morning. It seems he was pounding on the door when Frank got there.

'Sit down,' I said, 'and have a cup of tea.' He's a great one for tea. I was most friendly.

'Is my wife here, is my child here?' he said. My, my, my.

'They couldn't be,' said I. 'We were out to supper and we've just got in. Is there something wrong?' I sobered pretty smartly. Frank was walking around like a shop walker saying *he* was an honest man and would let no loose woman hide in his house.

'I warn you,' Eugene said. 'If she's here, you're culpable by law, for abducting my child.' The gripes. A raving encyclopedia of the law he was. I thought if this is how true love ends I'm glad I've never had the experience. He listed all her faults, you know, really intimate details that you wouldn't want known.

'By Christ,' said Frank, 'if she *is* here I'll have plenty to say to her, upsetting my night's sleep like this.'

'She isn't here,' I said. I had to be casual. The pair of them were stamping round all the time and I had visions of her creeping in, in a nightdress, saying, 'Did somebody call?'

'Look,' said I, coming the old honour, 'if she gets in touch with me I give you my oath that I'll ring you.' I'm amazing when I want to be. He made me repeat it, then left me a four-page letter for her, enumerating all her faults to her, and departed saying he'd use force if necessary. I saw him out, and boy did I chain that door after him.

Of course I had to tell Frank, I just had to. He nearly ripped the roof off. He tore up the stairs, with me after him, calling her name the way you'd call cows. She came out peppering.

'You get out of here,' Frank said. She pleaded to be left until morning. It was really debasing to see her pleading. He said no. He said he didn't want to end up in the divorce courts, thank you very much, and that he had his reputation to think of. I'd have injured him if capital murder wasn't operating in this country, and pig-faced ministers weren't screaming daily to bring back the birch. She looked as if she might die. I told him to go to bed and that she'd be gone before he got up. She and I spent the rest of the night figuring out where she'd go. I told her a bit – not too much – about the drummer's place and she began thanking me and slopping over me and I hate it when people thank you before-hand, because then it means you've *got* to help. Anyhow I rang hotels but none of them would have her. They were all full up. I suppose they thought she was a jail bird. So I had to try friends. Imagine ringing people at that hour of night and saying, 'I was just thinking of you. I just thought I'd ring up for a chat,' because of course I couldn't decently ask at once. They all said why didn't I have her. She was crying and supplicating and saying, 'Why did it have to happen to me?' Exactly my sentiments too. Because to tell you the truth I wasn't having all that much fun ringing people up in the middle of the night. Two lots banged the phone down on me.

'What was Eugene like, how did he look?' she kept saying. I said he looked shaken, naturally.

I said, 'You know what old Scott Fitzgerald said about the three o'clock in the morning state.' Giving her back one of her own tags. She's full of tags. Things that Scott said in bars, and wise saws that Ernest Hemingway gave out to whalers. As if she was their best friend and had breakfast with them on their ranches every morning.

Finally in the early morning I had to resort to blackmail. There's a crow who lives on our road and I let her keep her wheelbarrow in our treble garage, so I rang her. She wasn't one bit forthcoming. She hummed and hawed and I gave her the tune about a friend in need is a friend indeed, so she said, 'Well, maybe for a week or two.' She wouldn't hear of having the child because her dog bit kids.

'We'll have to put the kid in a kennel,' said I real sarcastic, and I fixed it that Kate would move in by eight in the morning and take her chances with the dog.

When I put the telephone down I knew what was coming. Remorse! As if I hadn't enough for one day. She pitied Eugene, she said. He was a misfit. He loved his child. She couldn't be responsible if he went mad. For whom the bell tolls. I mean I don't have to go over the rigmarole. You've heard it millions of times before.

The upshot is, her on the telephone to him, bursting over with apology and saying she shouldn't have done it. I thought after all that trouble I'd gone to, to get that room. She was so goddam servile I could have killed her. Telling him that he should have met a good woman, but that there was no such thing. Letting the sex down with a bang. The happy conclusion reached was that she'd bring Cash home and take the room herself, to brood over her faults for a few weeks.

'And we're still friends,' she kept saying. You could just imagine her saying that to a hangman.

We dressed the kid about seven and took him home. He was dead disappointed. He thought he was out for a month at least. We told him his mother had to go to hospital. The things kids are told! When we let him out and he trotted in his own path she looked after him and said, 'Poor Cash, he doesn't know what's ahead of him,' and that was the only time that I really made a fool of myself and cried. I mean he looked so harmless in the thick blue, gaberdine raincoat she had on him. And he turned around and grinned at us as if we were coming back in a few minutes.

'Parents,' she said.

'Parents,' I thought, the whole ridiculous mess beginning all over again. Hers and mine and all the blame we heaped on them, and we no better ourselves. Parents not fit to be kids. Talk of tears, we bawled and bawled and the driver had to go round the square twice before she was ready to go into her new lodgings. I couldn't go with her, it was too hurtful.

'How will I get through the day?' she asked.

'Have a sleep,' I said. You know, like, 'Have fun.'

'I can't.'

I knew 'twas unbearable for her but what could I do? What can anyone do for anyone else? I gave her 'Sweet dreams' pills and a few crisp fivers. These were the only times I found marriage at all pleasing – when I was handing out his money. Then to liven her up I said if she was going to do herself in, to be sure and make a will and leave me her diaries.

'I won't forget you, Baba,' she said, dead serious, dead dopey. I cannot stand serious people.

7

Later in the day I set to preparing for Harvey. I got the bedroom organized, removed our sleeping attire and Durack's toothbrush. It looks prehistoric, grey hairs soft and bushy and worn right down to the butt. He'll buy a helicopter but not a toothbrush. I then carted some of the more disastrous antiques to the shed. At four o'clock the old 'Home Sweet Home' door-bell chimed. God grant it's not Kate or a manure man, I thought. Once I was so bored I took pity on a manure man and bought stuff. Town manure stinks like nothing else you've ever dreamed of – what they add to it!

'All right, Mrs Cooney, I'll get it,' I said, real cool. That's our charwoman. She was halfway up the stairs but I beat her to the door and greeted him with a plastic smile. You won't believe it but he was standing there with a big drum and drumsticks and everything. It was very flash with red stones round the rim.

'It's not a concert,' I said. I didn't know what to say really.

'I thought you'd like to hear me play,' he said. Thought! He had a hell of a cheek bringing all that gear not knowing whether he'd get in or not, or whether he'd have to sneak out the pantry window in an emergency.

'Charming,' I said, bringing him into the room. I had a real hostess face on, and gold tights. He was in brown himself. Shirt, jacket, trousers – everything brown. I thought only someone really full of himself would wear such a boring colour and get away with it.

'You match the tobacco tones of the room,' I said, sarcastic.

'So?' he said, smiling. It was a grin really, a grin that said 'I can twist you around my little finger.'

Not me, baby, I thought as I watched him take a swig of the brandy I'd given him – we have all our grog bottled specially with our name on it.

Then he beckoned me to come over near him and I leapt across and he put his lips to mine and gave me brandy from his mouth. I nearly passed out with the thrill. I don't want to get all eejity about nature and stuff, but it was just like the way birds chew the food and then feed it in the mouths of their young. He could twist me around some barbed wire if he wanted to.

'Now sit down,' he said, 'and talk to me.' I went and sat on our studio couch with its patent floating comfort suspensions. 'Our playground,' I said, smiling. I thought he'd come and sit next to me but he didn't. He put a cushion on the floor, crossed his legs and sat like a mystic. He was looking around the room sizing it up.

'What's that crazy thing?' he said. It was an antique miniature coach that we carted one Sunday from Windsor.

'An antique – Queen Anne,' said I. I thought of the consignment of stuff out in the shed and what he'd make of that. But I was damned if I was going to get insulted in my own house. 'Being a garret man,' said I, 'you wouldn't probably know much about it.'

'I like simple wooden furniture,' said he.

'Gracious living,' said I, thinking of the orange boxes. We were really hitting it off.

'I'd love some more brandy,' I said then, meaning from the mouth. He got up and filled me a boring glass, and put it on the bamboo table in front of me. Durack read somewhere that bamboo was in, that Cecil Beaton had a bamboo whatnot in his studio, so he sent to Ireland to his poor old mother and got her to rake up all the bamboo in the place. Junk!

'Where are you from?' I said. I couldn't think of one witty thing.

'A nomad,' he said. Anyone else saying that would look a right fool, but not him. That was the thing about him. He wouldn't look a fool ever, no matter what he did. He had it all figured. He had the world by the short hairs too. He knew what to say but mostly it was a question of what not to say. No one would catch him out. There are people like that, quite a lot.

He said he'd lived all over; in Australia and Mexico and places and that he had Apache Indian blood. I thought how the hell can you be so white if you have Indian blood but that's not the sort of thing you can say. Indian blood is all the rage now.

'We'll have some tea,' I said and rang the bell although I hated to, but Cooney was so moody that if I didn't let her have a look in she mightn't show up for days. At least I warned her not to say the bit about 'keep your faith in God and your bowels open'. She says that to total strangers, like it was a recitation.

'Did you call me, madam?' she said, hopping in, in a clean apron, with the hat on. It's an atrocious hat with veiling but she thinks it does wonders for her. The 'madam' nearly killed me, she calls me by my Christian name, for God's sake, when we're alone. He started to smile and of course that gave her leeway to come in.

'Lovely drum,' she said. He said he was glad she liked it and would she like to hear him play.

'Oh, goody,' she says and sinks on to the couch with her stupid feet up in the air. Her legs are that short. He played some very earthy stuff, I mean 'twas loud and like the noise savages make with bones. We were a good audience. She was clapping like a maniac, I mean, clapping in the middle and places where she shouldn't. He was all intense and didn't pay attention to me once. That maddened me. I'd peeled off most of my underclothes and was freezing.

'Give us lavender blue,' Cooney said when he looked like stopping.

'I think we'll have tea, Mrs Cooney,' I said. She'd switched off. Strap. She has this hearing-aid. She can hear better than anyone but she got it for nothing on the health scheme. She's the sort would have her own teeth taken out just to avail of the free ones. I gave her a nudge in the ribs.

'Very nice of you, madam,' she said, and leaned over to the bamboo table and took a fistful of fags from the silver cigarette box. She put them all in her apron pocket except for the one she lit.

'Put a beggar on horseback and he'll ride to hell,' I said. She just ignored me and went on looking at his drumming. You'd think he was making love to that drum the way he brought it to life. He had his legs around it. She was clapping and humming. Finally I had to go make the tea myself. The tray was set for three but I removed one cup and saucer. When I came back into the room she noticed this straight away. She jumped up in a huff and shook hands with him and said he was a gentleman. She shot out of the room and came back almost at once with her coat on, saying in a toff's voice, 'Mrs Durack, I want a personal word with you at once.'

'I'm not at all pleased with you,' she said to me out in the hall. 'Discriminating like that as if I was black or something.'

'He's Indian himself,' I said just to confuse her.

'Jumped up Irish scum,' she said to me. A hell of a neck. She smelt like a brewery.

'I think you've had too much to drink,' said I. I knew that would kill her because although she tipples all day she never admits to drinking.

'No class! Letting me wash your knicks,' she said. I hoped to God he wasn't listening. It was all I needed to look alluring in his eyes. I opened the door and pushed her out.

'I know where I'm not wanted,' she said.

'It takes you a hell of a long time to register it,' I said. She put her head through the letter-box then, and began yelling and cursing and ringing the 'Home Sweet Home' bell. I came back into the room to find him half-way through the cucumber sandwiches and pouring himself another cup of tea.

'Are you all right?' I said just to let him know that I could see he was eating rapidly.

'Did the drumming excite you?' he said when I sat down.

'Oh, very much.' I was excited before ever he came.

'How?'

'Oh, you know how.'

'Where?'

'In my wooden leg.' Sweet Jesus, where did he think!

'Breasts or loins?' he said.

'Both.' I know roughly where your loins are, but I'd hate to have to point them out on a diagram.

'Good,' he said. He ripped into the cake and then a cigar from our box. Jokes – looking back on him he had the least sense of humour of anyone I ever met, and boy, I know some dull people. He dropped his previous cigarette butt into the great big china jardinière we have. It fizzled in there because there was water in the bottom since the last real flower display.

'Your husband's fetish,' he said, sort of sarcastic. True enough it did look like a great community chamber-pot but who was he to talk about fetishes.

We were getting nowhere.

'Come and sit near me,' I said.

'I prefer to look at you from here,' he said. 'The human face is not made for close-ups. There is only one time when it's bearable, that is,' he stopped as if he was going to say something revolutionary, for God's sake, 'on a pillow.'

'Plenty of pillows in the linen cupboard,' I said to be funny. I made a fool of myself twenty times per minute.

Then he stood up, took hold of one of the drumsticks and came over and started drumming me, mainly on the bosoms. Playful as hell. I don't know if you go in for that sort of thing but there's no fun in it. Merciful God. I just felt I was being pummelled.

'Turn round,' he said. I got a few on the bottom.

A thought struck me about my bruises. Frank often examines me, to see what the butler saw. I could see him inquiring about this mysterious mark and me saying, 'Waxed floor did it – I slipped,' and him saying, 'What waxed floor? We have fitted carpets,' and me saying, 'I took up a carpet to do it, houseproud little me, I even waxed the floor underneath.' A cock-and-bull story if ever I heard one.

Ouch, he went on drumming and boy did it hurt.

'I've studied the art of love-making since I was fourteen,' he said. He said he had his muscles under such control that he could make love to twenty-five women in an evening. He pointed to a little line of hair on his chin and said that it was put to use in love-making too.

'My hip bones, every part of me is brought to bear,' he said. Talk about the secrets of the orient. I was rearing to get upstairs.

Well, for the record we got up there about two hours later by which time you could have carried me on a stretcher I was so exhausted. 'Twas a ritual. I had to be drummed all over, then spin on my toes and play the damn drum with my fingers while he played it with his, and then kiss at a certain ordained moment, and not even got any pleasure out of it. 'Twas like drill at school. I had to act as if there was nothing happening. Not that there was that much going on.

'Now, one, two, three, begin,' he'd say. We had to keep time too. Talk about Pavlov's dogs. I'd have swapped with any of them.

'Will you do things for me?' he said upstairs as I clicked the Venetian blinds closed and drew the curtains. I locked the door.

'Do things!' I'd been working like a maniac for two hours.

'Have you a black brassiere?' he said. Of course I had. It's the only colour you don't have to wash every day. London is so filthy you'd be out of your mind to wear any other colour.

'And boots?' he said. 'Twas around the time that women

were wearing high leather boots to dinner parties and everything.

'No,' I said. ''Twas different for women that had legs like the back of a bus.

'You'll have to get some,' he said. 'And a leather coat.'

'I'll get Harrods to send the lot around, straight away,' I said. And then I blew a bit about how I'd heard they sent a van to Northumberland to deliver a biro pen and a rubber. He said not to bother for then, but to put on a sou'wester rain hat if I had one.

'And plenty of soap,' he said.

'Do you want basins of water too?' I said. I'm a pure slob. I mean I always think of soap and water together. 'Twas beginning to feel like a road accident. I got an old rain hat anyhow and left it on the pillow.

He took off his clothes and folded them real neat. I hate that. It means they're thinking more about not losing the crease in their trousers.

'Sorry about the boots and gear,' I said, 'but we'll have a rehearsal until such time as I get togged out.'

Not a smile out of him. I got undressed real snazzy. Quicker than the instructors that train firemen. I had so little on, for God's sake. He took one look at my skin and said 'twas too white. Just think of it. Unfortunate people hanged, drawn and quartered all over the world for being black and he had to say this. His own skin was pretty nice, smooth and sort of shiny like gold, polished wood with a line of hair down his stomach.

'Does this have a part in the mating ritual?' I said to the line of hair. Trying to get a bit of fun into it.

Well, I plugged in the old electric blanket and we plunged in.

'Have you ever had a woman?' he said.

'Plenty,' said I. I didn't know for a minute what he meant. I thought of getting it straight about booking the flat for Kate, but it could wait until the high jinks were over.

'Did you ever use milk bottles?' he said and then it struck me what he meant. So I said no, not at all, had he ever had a man?

'What makes you think that?' he said real huffy. I didn't think it. I thought nothing to tell you the truth except that we were taking a long time to do what millions of people do every hour of the day before they go to their work, or eat their breakfast or cut their toe-nails. I was beginning to have severe doubts. When he'd half smoked a cigarette he threw back the covers and began a light touch of singeing. You could smell it.

'Wait a minute,' says I. I'd have enough to account with the bruise marks beside having singed hair. Like an ill-plucked chicken.

'You'll like it,' he said. 'It will excite you.' Excite! I was about going out of my mind with excitement. I didn't like it. I knew some man that went in for that kind of frolic and giving women whiffs of ammonia and he ended up in clink and about ten of them ended up in their graves.

'Come on,' I said, putting the sou'wester on and getting all lovey dovey. He put the cigarette out and we got down to business.

'Is it big enough for you?' he said. Men worry about that a terrific lot.

'Enormous,' I said.

'You're a bright girl,' he said. Men are pure fools. Then the hip-bone bit came, which I took to be a mere preliminary and when I said he was welcome to press all, he said, 'It's gone to sleep.' They worry about that a terrific lot too.

He said that he wanted to kiss my teeth. I have two teeth on a brace, for God's sake. My teeth were the last things I wanted him to kiss. We lay quite still for a while and he said our bodies were as if a painter had flung them together on canvas. Did I like that? Did I think he was clever? I said yes to everything. I asked what things in the world he liked.

'The inside of a kitten's mouth,' he said. 'It's like water, only it's soft.'

Boy was he making me feel wanted. I asked him then what he was afraid of. I got really frantic to make conversation.

'That I'll lose any of my teeth,' he said. A born flatterer. I got the inference.

'And I'm afraid that I'm not as good a drummer as I think I am,' he said, then jumped up and looked at his wrist-watch which he'd left on the bedside table. He said he'd soon have to go because he was playing that night.

'I thought we were going to make love,' I said. Between you and me I really did.

'No,' he said, 'not today.' Then he said that I wasn't ready and that I talked too much.

'With me,' he said, 'it has to be pure. It has to be the most pure thing in the world, like the inside of a kitten's mouth.'

'I can see how you make love to twenty-five women in one evening,' I said to stab him. It worked like a dream. He got all virile then and with the aid of me, the sou'wester and himself he came out of his sleep and set to, to seduce me. We were engaged about four minutes flat when I heard him say, 'I came. I didn't think I would.'

'You're joking,' I said. By now I'd lost any notion I had that things were going to work out.

'You must promise me something,' he said then.

'Anything,' I said. He was that vain he didn't even notice the sarcasm.

'That you won't get pregnant,' he said.

'I'll try not to,' I said.

'But promise me,' he said. He was an imbecile. On second thoughts I was the imbecile. I suppose he thought with the tights and the elaborate bathrooms I knew all there was to know.

In about two seconds he got up and dressed himself and was all concentrated doing his tie knot in front of the mirror. I flung my clothes on, re-adjusted blinds and curtains, bashed the pillows a bit and smoothed the bottom sheet. Things weren't very tossed anyhow. He wouldn't wait for coffee, just got me to ring for a taxi and then, real surprised, banged his pockets and found he had no money.

'Loan me a pound,' he said. I gave him nineteen and eleven just to see if anything would wring a laugh out of him.

'About the studio for Kate?' I said, out on the front steps. I wanted to fix another appointment, to keep things going. Because although he bored me he didn't bore me all that much.

'Sure,' he said. 'I'll ring you tomorrow,' and then he made his big joke by punching me in the stomach, showing me what pals we were. The taxi came and he lifted the drum down the steps and said was it all right to leave the gate open because he couldn't manage to fasten it. I closed the hall door before the taxi moved off.

I felt awful, I can't tell you how awful I felt. One thing I knew, I was going to be saddled with all this guilt and I not having a bit of enjoyment out of it, only exertion. I rang Brady to tell her the flat wouldn't be ready for a few days but she wasn't there. Out drowning herself, I imagined.

*

Cooney didn't come next morning. There was an impudent note stuck under the door to say she wanted her cards and compensation.

'What does this mean?' Frank said. He opens my letters. He was in a flaming humour, trying to put on his cuff links.

'Oh, one of her moods,' I said. 'You know how she is.'

'That's no answer,' he said. He'd smelt a rat already because when he came home the evening before I was carting the stuff in from the coal house.

'What in the hell are you doing?' he said. 'That's valuable mahogany furniture I'll have you know.'

'Just french-polishing it,' said I. The stuff was covered with coal dust.

Then he went to the sink and saw the two good cups, saucers and plates.

'Who was here?' he asked.

'A poor old man,' I said. I couldn't think of one person's name.

'I'll have to go and speak to Mrs Cooney,' I said, doing the second cuff-link for him. We were having a dinner party that night, the brother and his wife, an architect, and some big merchant that they were soft-soaping to get a deal out of.

'How many courses?' he said.

'About five.' I hadn't a clue what we were having. I hadn't given it a thought, you can imagine why.

'Don't forget about the cranberry sauce,' he said.

He got cranberry sauce in some house and he thinks it's the biggest deal he ever had.

'You can't have cranberry sauce unless you have turkey,' I said.

'Well bloody well have turkey,' he said. 'Have two turkeys.'

'A cock and a hen?' I said. I was as briary as hell.

'None of that smut,' he said, lifting a hair-brush. I skipped away in case it developed into a fracas. He shouted something going out and I knew that he'd take revenge by yelling at bogmen that are no better than himself.

At about half ten the brother's wife rang to know was it dress. Imagine a bunch of us tripping each other up in long frocks in our own front room.

'Wear anything you like,' I said. I was looking up the directory to see if the drummer was listed. I was going to ask him when Kate could move in. Very obvious tactics.

'What are you wearing?' she said. She thinks of nothing else. Someone could tell her a story of a woman that was raped and murdered on Waterloo Bridge and she'd say, 'What was she wearing?'

'Any old thing,' I said.

'That's fine,' she said, 'I'll do the same. I'm glad it's nothing elaborate.'

'Well, I had better get a move on,' I said.

'What's Lady Margaret wearing?'

'How would I know?'

Lady Margaret was the only titled person him and the brother knew. They got in with her for giving monumental subscriptions to some charity organization that she championed. Bitches like that take up charity to get their photos in the paper. Good thing he met her because before that we had a bit of a catastrophe with a duchess. We went to the local pub when we first moved to here because it said outside 'Dine and drink like a King' and he liked that. Anyhow there was a woman there that everyone called the Duchess. She was a gas card, all wrinkles and rouge, and one of those eejity coats with a flared skirt and fur collar. The minute he heard one of the boys calling her Duchess he got real interested.

'We ought to offer her a drink,' says he. She was knocking back gins like nobody's business. Well, he didn't dare approach her that night, but next night he said we'd go around again and I knew what he was aiming at. We hung around that bar for hours and she came in with a couple of midgets that were probably jockeys.

'She probably has a few good tips for the Grand National,' he said.

'So have you,' I said. I hated to see him that desperate to get in with anyone.

Every time a tray of drinks was brought to her table he'd look over. He was plucking up courage. Finally he sent over a round just before closing time and she raised her glass and beckoned us to come over.

'Cheers, Duchess,' he said. She lapped that up. We all got introduced, and then he said why didn't they come back with us for a drink. I was in my own kitchen making Irish coffee for them when he burst out:

'Christ Almighty,' he said, 'it's a nickname. She's not a real duchess at all.'

I burst laughing into his face.

'Get her out of here,' he said. 'She might flog the silver!'

'Well, watch her,' said I. *I* couldn't very well throw her out.

'Watch her! I can't face her again. I asked her what her crest was, and she said, "Mop and Pail, governor."'

'Is the Monseigneur coming?' my sister-in-law asked. I said of course. Frank won't tile a roof until he's discussed it with the Monseigneur. She hates it that the Monseigneur is more friendly with us than with them. I could just see him beside the fire, raving away about you can't beat an open fire, and full of well-being from the Double Cream Sherry. Suffer the decanter to come unto me. I really was in a hell of a humour.

'Must go,' I said to the sister-in-law. 'See you later.' The drummer wasn't listed so I decided to give him a day and if he hadn't rung me by then I'd drive up next day and bring Brady as a homeless orphan. I rang and told her.

'I can't sleep,' she said. 'I can't eat. I keep going over and over it.'

'Get out,' I said. 'Get an interest.'

'In what?' she said. I began to rack my brains. Mother of Jesus, I don't know why I was worrying about her when I had me to worry about. I was really stuck on that drummer.

One can't be tough all the time. My tea-cup looked ominous too. I told Brady we were having a dinner party and if she wanted any scraps she could come around to the back door, for the leavings. First she said she didn't eat, then she said she had some pride left, and thirdly she had indigestion. I hung up after I'd promised to talk to her later, to mend her life, to get old Eugene gone on her again, to fix an audience with the Pope, and some last suppers with wise, beneficent men.

'I'll make it up to you, Baba,' she said. I'd been hearing that particular tune from her, in that particular tone of voice, for about twenty years now. I was tired of it.

I said, 'See you later.'

I had to go after Cooney and make a real servile fool of myself.

She had to get two lots of fivers as a bribe: one to keep her mouth shut about Drummer boy and the other to come over and cook the dinner. I wouldn't know what side to lay a turkey on.

'Did he stay late,' says she, 'your pianist?' She knew well he wasn't a pianist. She was just trying to get me to contradict her so that we would have another row and I'd dole out more fivers.

'He was working,' said I. 'He left soon after you.'

'I was thinking when I saw the curtains drawn that you'd hardly have gone to bed with him downstairs drumming.'

'Hardly,' I said. I was opening tins like a maniac – cranberries, blueberries, all sorts of berries. I'm a dab hand at opening tins.

'Lovely drum,' she said. 'Lovely instrument. I wouldn't say no to one for Christmas.'

I can take a hint as well as anyone.

We worked like troopers all day and I kept a chair to the kitchen door so that I'd hear the telephone ringing in the hall.

'You're a bundle of nerves,' she said.

'For a stupid woman you have great perception,' I said. Anyone could see I was a bundle of nerves. I broke three glasses, and cutlery was flying out of my hand as if I was a goddam medium in some poltergeist play. We got things more or less right anyhow, and she did some snazzy sauces. If only she wasn't so low I'd have liked her.

At seven they started arriving. Lady Margaret first. Linked up the steps by her chauffeur as if she was a cripple or something.

'Midnight,' she said, and he tipped his hat and went off. Her boots were full of snow and she had to change of course and the hall was ruined with puddles. You'd think it was a little doggie or something.

'Any little Duracks on the way?' she said to me upstairs. She always said that to me when she got me upstairs, and I always said I thought there were. Just to get her off it. She took ages to do her hair, and put more stuff on her face that was already like enamel. She said her mink had been dyed to a colour that no other mink in the British Isles could approach.

'You should get one – not like mine of course,' she said.

'I will,' I said. 'There's tons of them at the railway lost property offices.' Honest to God, I'd seen notice boards about it. Ranch mink and wild mink and blue mink. She didn't like that, I could see by the way she hurried out of the bedroom and down the spiral stairs in a hurry.

'Maggsie,' Frank said, glorying in it. It's a phoney name he invented to make it seem they're old school chums. She gave him one of those non kisses that dressed-up women give. You know, touch-me-not. I went to the door again because the little architect had arrived. She was nice enough, and took her plastic over-shoes off in the hall and made no big fuss about going upstairs to view herself. The big merchant was almost on her heels and he asked me if I got the flowers before I had a chance to thank him. White chrysanthemums came. I had them on show of course, and the room looked quite happy with all of us apparently having a gay evening, and Frank standing next to me with his arm on my shoulder. Proprietary. Married bliss. Big fire burning in the granite fireplace. Bottles of red wine stood near to warm up; white wine getting chilled. Don't think we got that information for free – I took a course along with the dreariest collection of women you could summon up.

Cooney was banging saucepans like hell down in the kitchen and Frank was coughing before getting on with the two stories he'd planned to tell. It was a month when everyone had a cough or a head cold and catarrh sounds orchestrated the hectic conversation.

'You won't believe it,' he said, 'but I met a man today and he has three hundred and sixty-five shirts. One for every day of the year.'

'He needs one extra for the leap year,' said I to the little architect girl who looked as if she might be realizing what a vile evening she'd let herself in for.

The thing about Frank and the brother is they hire nice people. They have boys who would sit up all night on that building site just to make sure that buckets aren't stolen. Now and then they get what Frank calls a hobo on the site. Someone with a bit of common sense that knows about unions and strikes and things. And boy, do they have *him* fall off a scaffold!

'And after he's worn his shirt once,' Frank was saying, 'he has it beautifully laundered by the French nuns.' There's a posh laundry where nuns hand-wash and hand-iron shirts at vast expense. Must be tough on the poor nuns never having a date with any of the men.

'And then?' the Monseigneur was saying with interest. I could see he was planning to get to know this man and give religious instructions in lieu of shirts.

'Well, Monseigneur,' Frank said – he calls him by his name every couple of seconds – 'this is where the shrewdness comes in: then he sells them to other men who are not so rich. I mean wealthy men in their own right, but not rich beyond the dreams of avarice.'

'Well, it's a good thing, a wholesome thing,' the

Monseigneur said. 'After the loaves and fishes, Our Lord asked them to gather up the leavings. Waste is not a Christian ethic either.' Then he made a big joke: he moved very close to Frank and looked at his thick neck and said, 'Would I be right in thinking, Frank, that you're wearing one yourself?' Everyone looked then.

'Monseigneur, you're a caution,' Frank said. 'Having me on like that.'

Frank was wearing a four-pound-fifteen-shilling striped job got in the King's Road. I could still see that impotent bastard in his brown attire, strutting around the room.

'That's how to keep one's money,' Lady Margaret said. She managed to keep her own fairly intact. She had a big place in Ireland with butlers and all that, but God, had she rotten legs. Even in the evening skirt which she was wearing you'd know she had bad legs.

'Baba, what sort of hostess are you? Their glasses are empty, empty!' Frank said. He was gathering wind for his second story.

'Don't we know where it is and that we're welcome to it,' the Monseigneur said, helping himself. I was well oiled before the brother and his wife came. She was in a white crocheted creation. It really shook me because I was in one of my ordinary things. I hadn't the incentive to dress if you want to know. I knew Frank would be livid, because the competition between him and brother is desperate. The way it is between good friends.

'I know someone who wants to catch her death,' I said, because her back was exposed right down to her middle.

'I simply had to show it to you,' she said. 'It was flown over today.' I didn't even ask from where but anyhow she was a big hit with all and sundry. I hustled them to the dining-room before nine because I had some mad idea about nipping out to find him after they'd all gone.

Cooney conducted herself very well throughout the dinner. For one thing she didn't wear that hat or get chatting. There was one tricky second when they began to compliment me on the food. She had her revenge though, she thrust a boiling hot sauce boat into my hand and sailed away.

'Cranberry sauce,' Frank kept saying. 'More turkey, Maggsie. More ham, anybody?'

'You can't beat the Irish ham,' the Monseigneur said. 'The succulence of it.'

Succulence! It was straight from Denmark.

Then they got on to food and how poor they'd all been at one time or another. You know, vying with each other to know who had starved the oftenest. The merchant, who hadn't opened his mouth up to then, told a big rigmarole about walking around London with one and threepence in his pocket and standing outside cafés trying to decide to have a one-and-threepenny meal and no evening paper, or a shilling meal and a paper for the racing results.

'Indeed I did,' he said, looking around for their reactions.

'I believe it,' Frank said.

'Until the bank opened,' I said, real bitchy. He got all flustered then and Lady Margaret made some sort of disapproving sound, as if she was spitting out pips.

'Baba has a good heart,' I heard the Monseigneur say. 'Her only failing is that she inclines to be outspoken.'

Frank butted in to tell them how good I was to the poor and how I'd given a beggar man tea from one of the good cups. That of course set me thinking about my drummer again. I could just see him dropping the cigarette into the big, vulgar, china pot. And the way he had of throwing a match away. He held it between his thumb and middle finger and dismissed it like an arrow. I was miles away most of the time. I thought one week of him and I'd be bored but boy, would I do anything for that one week. I'd buy boots the following day and a coat like he said and one of those rain hats.

'She's not to give in to fatalism, is she, Baba?' the Monseigneur was saying. Eliciting sympathy from me for the Maggsie cow.

'I don't know,' said she, the arch phoney that she is, 'whether to drown myself in my beautiful lake or marry my butler.' She had a lake in Ireland and a butler from Italy and I'd heard that piece of timed despair before. I was about to say, 'Go up the river on a bicycle,' when the telephone rang. Brady, I thought. So I skipped across to one of the occasional tables and picked it up, prepared to say, 'Don't get on a moaning bout.' Sweet Jesus, it was him.

'Would you like to come down to the Serpentine and have a swim?' he said.

'Who's that?' I'd know his low voice in hell.

'Would you?'

'Strictly for the ducks,' I said. God Almighty, the whole crew of them had their necks and ears craned. You know the way people pretend to be talking but aren't really, well that's what they were doing. I couldn't go to one of the four extensions either because I knew his Lordship would pick it up. I turned my back on them, not that it helped.

'So you don't want to come?' he said. Christ, was he touchy!

'Are you coming over tomorrow?' I said. It was dead difficult to say things that he'd understand and they wouldn't catch on to. Anyhow I'm no use at it.

'It's doubtful,' he said.

'Well when?' I said. I was taking terrible risks.

'Come to the Serpentine, baby,' he said. I was afraid of my life they'd hear what *he* was saying.

'Tomorrow,' I said and stopped as if I had nothing else to say.

'Well, don't forget I asked you,' he said and we hung up more or less together. I was shaking all over.

'Who's that?' Frank said.

'Just a friend,' I said as cool as a breeze.

'Who is it?' he said – stubborn again. The brother, that shark with the blood pressure, was giving me the eye too, as much as to say, 'We're powerful and you can't lie to us.' The vote, I thought, means nothing to women, we should be armed.

'My dentist,' said I. 'I missed out on an appointment.' I hadn't even got one in England. I got the brace and things in Ireland.

Cooney came in with the coffee and looked at me, real interested. She knew it all and recognized his voice of course.

'Mrs Cooney, you've been simply marvellous,' I said to give her a bit of puff. She beamed.

'A pleas-ure,' she said. We were well matched.

The thing went on for hours. They got to the Pope and Khrushchev.

'He's afraid of his life of the Pope,' the brother said.

'So well he ought,' said his wife. 'His Holiness could wipe him out.'

'Now, now, now, don't give our friend the wrong impression,' the Monseigneur said. Our friend the merchant was a Protestant and doing very nicely with the brandy and the sister-in-law's back to explore. He didn't give two pins about the Pope but he felt he had to say something.

'A point I've often wanted to raise with you chaps,' he said, 'do priests wear trousers under their cassocks?'

Even in the state I was in, I roared out laughing. Everyone else got very red in the face and nervous but the Monseigneur replied as if he wasn't shocked at all. You know, nothing-shocks-me sort of thing.

They covered crime too and unmarried mothers and the morals of England. As if the morals of Ireland were any better. About twenty hours went by before their various chauffeurs and taxis came, and they were hardly out of the door before I was up the stairs to bed.

'I'm worn out,' I said to Frank. I could not have endured intimacy that night. He looked very satisfied. He said he'd made two jokes and did I notice how everyone laughed? He said the merchant looked as if he would come through. Everything looked rosy except that I had to get to see my drummer, or die.

Next morning I ripped up there and brought Brady as an alibi.

'I hope it's a nice place,' she kept saying. 'Congenial.' Everything had to be congenial.

'I hope we get in,' I said. I knew he'd be a bit huffed about my not going to the Serpentine for an orgy but I had a few things to cheer him up: some smoked salmon for brek and the biggest pair of boots you ever saw. I looked like a general in them.

We got through the front door because it was wide open and we climbed as many flights as I remembered having climbed. There were no names on any of the doors. 'Twas one of these sleazy dives where people didn't want their names on doors in case they'd be found out. Hashish, pep-pills, pimping, all kinds of contemporary offences. Brady's face was a study. I got a look at it on the landing, with the foul light that came through the skylight.

We got to his door. I recognized the brass mermaid knocker.

'Smoked salmon?' I said as the door opened back. A woman faced me. An ordinary-looking crow in black.

'Is Harvey in?' I said.

'Who?' she said.

'Harvey,' I said. She was a born evader.

'Oh, Harvey,' she said, as if I'd been talking in double Dutch.

'Yes, him,' I said, glaring at her.

'We've come about the flat,' Eejit Brady said, telling our business. She always tells her business to everyone.

'I own the flat. He was living here,' she said, the smug cow.

'Oh no,' said Kate, as if that's what we'd really cared about.

'Can you give me Harvey's address? I want to return his piano,' I said.

'I can't,' she said. 'He didn't leave a forwarding address.'

The nomad jag had stuck in my mind. He was gone. We stood there a few more minutes and then shuffled off.

All that day we tried restaurants and clubs, because I knew he played in some dive. Sharks asked us would we like to audition for strip-tease, and one told me I had the makings of a lady wrestler. There wasn't a trace of him. I even rang the boring actor whose mother was on solvents, but he knew nothing. He didn't even know *my* name, for God's sake.

'Did you know him well?' Brady kept asking. She couldn't

understand why I was so hot and bothered. He'd got my arse in an uproar and left me high and dry. I more or less knew he'd skipped. Like a fool I went to the Serpentine to see if he was there. Useless. The ducks got the smoked salmon, bag and all.

8

Kate's room turned out to be small but adequate. A single bed, a wall cupboard and a wash-basin that lurked behind a green cretonne curtain. The curtain had a smell of dust, as curtains have when they are not laundered for years. From the hot tap cold water came, and from the cold tap hottish water came, and she knew that when she left the place, as she eventually must, it was this detail she would remember – the folly of the reversed taps. In the mornings she cooked her breakfast in the kitchen – the lower shelf of the cupboard being allotted to her foodstuffs – and carried it back up to her bedroom to eat it there, saluting the dog or the landlady if she met either, appeasing them both with a smile before vanishing into her cell once again. At nine she went to work. She had taken a part-time job in a cleaners, which meant she earned some money and did not have to take charity from Eugene. To be maintained by a man who did not love her was depraved. Not that he'd offered! She had afternoons free. Sometimes she walked, or saw Baba, and on three afternoons she met Cash. They would go to some park or other and she would ask him questions about what went on at home.

'Oh, boredness,' he said, a word he'd made up.

'Like what?' she said, breaking all the rules of decency.

He never told, he merely gathered fistfuls of snow to fling at her, or when she ducked and protested, at some uncomplaining tree stump. After a few flings he would grumble about his cold hand, and removing the wet glove she would warm the hand finger by finger, licking each one back to life again. He liked that. He even seemed happy. But at times, looking into his over-white face and his over-liquid, dark eyes with the mauve shadows (from constipation), she would think that he knew everything that was happening, and everything that would happen in the future. They always went to a café for tea – the same one each time because she knew the prices – and he ate chips, and éclairs filled with mock cream. Sometimes he shed a few tears when they were leaving.

On one such afternoon after she had delivered him to Maura at a bus stop she found his glove in her pocket and knowing he had only one pair she decided to deliver it to the house later that night. When she got there it was about eight, but the curtains were not drawn – one of Eugene's many liberation schemes. The family – Maura, Cash and Eugene – were at the dinner table. The double doors separating front and back rooms were also open so that she could see right through to the place where she once sat, and where the girl now replaced her. There was music from the record player, Russian dance music that he often played because he said it suggested happy, jingly, Russian people dancing about in the snow. She could see Maura's face and Cash's, and two mouths moving, and the back of his still head, and she put her nose to the window to try and catch some word of what they said. Suddenly she noticed a figure to one side of her, in front of the garage door. At first she thought it was real and was about to run, shamefaced. It was a snowman, about the height of Cash, and going to it she saw his size and his features exactly reproduced: the round face with the cheeks that hollowed ever so slightly, the big, bullet head, and a little stub of a branch for his nose, as small and neat as his own nose. Eyes had been traced there too, big eyes: a perfect likeness. Maura must have done it while he was out, as a surprise for when he got back. Kate kept looking at it for a long time, and she could see it perfectly because the moon was full and the whiteness of gardens and hedges and gate piers gave to this figure an uncanny presence. It might not melt for days. She wanted to pick it up and carry it off, but daren't.

The glove was still her reason for coming. She thought of leaving it on the pier, where children's lost gloves are always left, but since the snow would ruin it she stuck it through the letter-box, but did not let it drop through, in case one of them might hear. Maura had remarkable hearing.

Then she ran until she was out of breath and had to stand. She had not been back to the neighbourhood in weeks. Already it looked strange. The full moon and the dazzle of stars put a spell on the little houses, the powdered street and the glassy pond where she'd long ago fed the ducks and swans. It was a dance floor now with branches touching its surface, those laden down by their weight of snow. She stepped on the ice, first one foot, then another. She wanted to walk there, and dance there, for ever, with her son or with his image which had been reproduced by someone else. If only she could do that and lose herself, the way one reads of young girls dancing alone with roses held between the teeth. But her thoughts kept going back to the three of them, in the warm room, beyond the iced-over window, the snow-child outside, keeping guard.

In a way it was the worst night of all.

One thing Eugene had instilled in her was the need to have a walk each day, and walk she did no matter what the weather. It thawed and refroze all the time. Dykes of grey snow were piled in the gutters and the tyres of buses sloshed this swept snow around her booted ankles. She could hear icicles, cracking like girders, and women going by grumbling about the shortage of plumbers. She went to a park. Flowers were out – a few, tatty, forlorn crocuses, but they were flowers all the same and they meant something. She sat at her appointed seat and saw him come and knew then why she had come back. He was a young boy who came in the cleaners' every Friday with his skin-tight, dirt-tight jeans to avail himself of the two-hour service. He sat next door – in last season's jeans – in the café, and after the two hours rivved home to change into his renewed, Romeo, silver-grey ones.

She'd met him the day before in the park and he called out 'Gorgeous' after her. Gorgeous – with a body shapeless from extra clothing, and a face stricken by all that had happened. But she acknowledged it all the same.

He was with a friend now. They rode their bicycles over the snowy grass, making crazy patterns, looping around, then swerving and re-patterning their tracks. And all the time shaking the handlebars at each other as matadors would wave a cape at a bull. Gradually coming closer and closer until they surrounded the bench on which she sat. She was on a bench in the middle of a park, her legs a little apart, her eyes looking beyond them at the square concrete factory with its honeycomb of square windows and a sign beginning with H commanding the horizon. The same H that she saw at night, instead of a moon. Their eyes ran up and down the length of her legs which were covered with blue wool stockings. She did not look at them observing her but she knew that they were. A secret flutter took possession of her as if a bird had come between her legs and flown high up under her coat and thick tweed skirt. He made a sucking noise, the one who'd called her gorgeous. He was pale with very drained blue eyes and spots that just missed being pimples. He wore a silver chain so tight around his neck that it could choke him. The second boy had Italian blood and they both had long hair curling on the napes of their necks. She had not looked at them as they circled the bench, but she knew their faces from the cleaners'.

'New type of kissin' come in,' the pale boy said as he cast his bicycle from him and lay belly downwards on the snowy grass, facing her. He had his head raised, his elbows dug into the snow and he scratched with his thumb at the medal on the chain. His eyes ran up the length of her legs. Could he see the knickers too? The warm, chaste, winter knickers with long legs, elastic reinforced.

If she said, 'Go away,' he could have said, 'Belt up, I pay rates too,' so she said nothing only stared straight ahead at the H which would soon be a moon-bright neon. He called to his friend, 'Git, there's a gorgeous bird that works in a bread shop, a real doughnut.' His friend roared off saying, 'Don't tempt the girl. Can't ye see she's contemplatin'.'

Kate crossed her legs and locked them at the ankles, like a lady sitting down to tea in a convent parlour where she'd once sat with abstemious nuns sitting around her, watching. He screwed up his face, frowned with his red-rimmed eyes, and rolled his half-nourished, humble little body over and over again on the dirty snow. His jeans would need longer in the vat next Friday. She felt shame because she knew she had yielded to him for an instant the week before. That was when she unfolded his trousers and asked if he wanted it 'Express' with something more than behind-the-counter pleasantness. A madness had passed through her limbs and shone in her eye. But now the bird between her legs died. Quicker in fact than it had taken for the blob of snow that was on her upturned collar to melt. It was trickling down her neck now, worrying her. She thought, I could easily put my hand out and let him draw me down and give him something that would briefly atone for the condemned room where he was born and the stupid parents he came out from and the accent he is doomed to. She glanced with mild pity to say this without actually saying it.

'Fabulous out of doors,' he said.

'It's cold,' she said stiffly, being careful to misunderstand him.

'Git your knees apart, mine aren't half warm.'

'How dare you,' she said, the voice of a lady brigadier, a gym mistress, a hospital matron, the voice of authority pealing down through the centuries. Where had she got it from? Her legs and knees trembled, and she stood up and raced across the field with her heart falling out of her mouth.

'How about puttin' the matter to your solicitor,' he called after her, and then his friend shot back from nowhere and she heard the pale boy say, 'Them dirty married bags,' and the epithet cut and carried across the desolate field. She hurried to the Ladies' lavatory that was behind some soot-black arbour trees shrill at that moment with starlings. Inside, the Dettol smell, the unwiped lavatory seat, the roller without a towel and the attendant without a smell-sense depressed her not for their own sake but because of her transgression. A week before she had led him on. As she unfolded his dirty, silver-grey jeans she had some notion of having a vague and magic encounter, of being taken by him, and then left satiated as he tore away. Not knowing his first name or what occupation his dirt-engrained hands were put to. Not knowing anything. A voice from outside called Paul, roughly, and with anger, Paul, Paul.

'Somebody's calling Paul,' the attendant said.

The following Friday Kate stayed away sick.

After that she went for walks only in the evening when the fog was coming down. She did not have to look people in the eye and the river was at its best under gauze, with green lights denoting the passing of some boat. To reach the park that skirted the river, she had to pass a street of houses. Fine houses set back from the road, with ivy, with studio windows, and one with an inked sign saying 'Beware, very slippery path'. Solid fortifications with beware people inside leading solid lives. Powerful smells of roast and gravy came out to trouble her. She had had mutton or beef stew depending on the day. One-gas-ring, one-saucepan dinner! Funny that she should remember meals they had eaten more clearly than she remembered anything else. Especially cere-monial ones like the hen pheasant that had got caught by mistake in a rabbit trap. They roasted it, and he'd stuck one of the russet feathers through her auburn hair and joked about not having to buy her a present. It was near her birthday. How could they renounce all of that? She hurried home, sat on her bed, resting the writing-pad on her knee, and wrote:

My dear Eugene,

I don't know if it will make reparation but I want
to say that the affair I had was foolish and trite. When
I recall his letters now – the ones you have – I feel
nothing but shame. Of course I did you wrong but I
did myself wrong too. I have a screw loose, that screw
which should let me know when I was on solid ground
and stop me wading into a swamp. I do not know why
I do bad things.

She signed it 'Little Kate'. A harking back to the early
days.

She said nothing about the years of emotional pummel-
ling from him, or her own compulsion to love on an octave
note from one daybreak to the next. She posted it but did
not expect an answer, and when she got one two mornings
later she trembled as she opened the brown business envelope and unfolded the sheet of foolscap. He wrote:

Dear Kate,

What I have to do now is forget about little Kate
(what a misnomer) and get on with those parts of my
life which I have so foolishly neglected because of her.

His investment in her had been too much. She would
never be free of the responsibility for the waste of his life.
She read it twice and let it go into the Thames where she
was standing once again. Another evening. The tide-marks
lost in the gloom. Too late. She knew the letter off by heart
like a prayer. If only she had the decency to kill herself.
Water was the gentlest way to suicide. It merely meant
stepping off the path on to another path that was equally

blurred by mist. As her mind dwelt on it her body ran from that place and walked through the High Street, peering into the jocularity of pubs, looking at clothes she had no desire to own, at plastic chickens motionless on skewers and printed signs to testify that lambs' tongues were cheaper by fourpence. Ugly streets, ugly signs. She walked for a long time with the bouquet of frying oil in her nostrils, crossing over and back, comparing the prices in one window with those in another, longing to crash through one of those windows, as she had once seen a boy do on a drunken Saturday night. But the police would come and take her away in a big black van and things would be no better.

That night – or perhaps it was another night, because all those nights were interchangeable – she had a dream: Cash was asleep, no bigger than a baby, in a cot, with a napkin bagging down around his knees. She went to Maura and asked her to kill the child by burning him with an iron. Maura did. Cash died quietly, without a whimper. It had obviously been painless. She saw a little blood on the napkin, but that image had been borrowed from real life when he was circumcised as an infant and carried back to her from the operating theatre. There had been a little rosette of blood on the napkin and she wept because he had known pain in his unknowing, unsuspecting milk-happy euphoria. She did not waken then, screaming, as she would have expected to. The dream went on. She lived through months, years, running out of restaurants, furniture shops, hairdressers, sick with pain because she had killed the only person she was capable of loving. She eventually would have to go to Eugene and say, 'I killed our child. It wasn't an accident, I killed him.' She wakened then, and having no thought for time or sleep she went out to the telephone on the landing and dialled Eugene's number.

'How is Cash?' she asked.

'Are you drunk?' he asked, his voice wide awake. Was he in bed? On which side? Did he ever waken and think she was still lying next to him, pink and warm in her fleece-lined nightgown?

'Is he all right?' she asked again.

'He's asleep. He had some hot milk about two hours ago.'

'I had a terrible dream about him,' she said.

'Must be indigestion, take two aspirins.' She did not put the phone back on the receiver, she just pushed it away from her and laid it on the ledge where it went on emitting sounds until he realized he was talking to nothing and hung up.

Next day she said 'Shit' to a bus conductor who refused her change of a pound. She knew everything that was happening but could not help herself.

Then Cash lost a front tooth. He seemed so empty, so stripped without it that when she met him she asked where his prettiness had gone. He said the tooth fell out and they had put it in an eggcup and he got sixpence. She could see the sixpence shining silver in the water and Cash putting in his finger to prize it out.

'I want Cash's tooth,' she said to his father a few hours later when he was picking up the child at the railway station. So much of her life centred on that platform that she knew all the advertisements off by heart and the telephone numbers of places to ring if one needed God or tranquillity or lessons in ballroom dancing. She was familiar with the various obscene messages and pencil changes done to the posters. A girl displaying a man's outsize shirt had been given a moustache, and a lipstick queen had had one eye cut away.

'The tooth is perfectly safe,' Eugene said. 'I've put it away for him when he grows up.'

'I want it,' she said.

'Now don't get all emotional, it's safe.'

'I must have it,' she said. It was not the tooth at all.

She got it eventually and put it in her purse but lost it. She must have handed it between the folds of a pound note in some transaction or other. She asked in two shops but without luck. She never forgave herself.

'I lost your little hollow tooth, I'm sorry,' she said to Cash when they met again. Cash didn't care. She was gloomy and squeezed him too tight and asked who he loved the most. Not like Maura. Maura played fox and goose and smelt like a mother and had hair between her legs just like a mother too. He saw her through the keyhole. She nearly split her sides laughing. Maura laughed a lot and his mother cried a lot. He'd have another loose tooth soon and get another sixpence. He tried to shift one with his finger but it would not wobble. He loved that wobble feel until it got looser and looser and was held on by one thread of gum.

'What are you doing, Cash?' his mother asked. He always had a finger in his mouth.

'Nothing,' he said.

Did Maura or his father ever talk about her?

'I forget,' he said.

'Try and remember.'

'Dada said you're jealous of other people's belly buttons.'

'What?'

He repeated it. She tried to get him to remember when, and where, and how. But he could not or would not trace it

91

for her. He made a face and said, 'Big fat sausage,' so that she would chase him and tickle him the way she used. He ran around the playground but she remained on the wooden seat, staring at, but not seeing the motionless swings, the squat, un-horse-like wooden horse and the sandpit covered over with snow.

'Mama,' he called. She did not rise. Other mothers had arrived so she could not question him. And she did not hop about on the chalked squares to warm her feet either, because of formality. The mothers were supposed to sit and watch the children play. Once when she'd got on the swings the attendant came over and asked her was she over sixteen, and if so, to please get off.

'I got locked in this park one night,' a mother was saying. 'No!' from another.

'I did, I climbed over that gate.'

They were enclosed by high wire-netting and by a wired gate. How had that ungainly woman mounted the gate? What breathing and puffing must have gone on? Did she disturb the leaves? Some falling leaves had never reached the ground but had got caught in the wire and were fixed there now, like decoration. Not in clusters but separate. They reminded one of something. Spring and childbirth? Autumn and rotting? So he discussed her faults. It was not enough to kill her, he had to show the sad spectacle of her corpse to others.

'I got across to the main gate,' the woman was saying, 'and I called a couple going by. "I'm locked in," says I, and they wouldn't believe me. They thought I was Candid Camera. "Don't you heed her," his girl said to him. "You'll find there's a camera behind the bushes and you'll see your-self on television next week, being ridiculous."'

'Wicked,' her listless listener said.

'Mama.' It was Cash again. He was walking through the maze nodding to the wooden posts as if they were people. She went over to him.

'Did you know that some people believe the earth is flat?'

'I suppose they do.' She felt bad-tempered, because she couldn't probe about what his father said.

'Yes, they belong to the earth-is-flat club. Can I have a club?'

'Do.'

'A what club?'

'Ask them.' She was staring at two children, one white and one coloured, who were enacting the birth of a baby on the slide. The coloured girl stood at the bottom and pushed a life-size doll up the slide and the little mother at the top slid down with the doll between her parted legs and the midwife took it from her. They had done it five times.

Cash went over, stood near, and the pause, typical of children, took place, while they vetted each other, and then spoke. The coloured child left with Cash when the closing-time bell pealed out. Her name was Tessa.

'I have a radio of my own,' Tessa was telling him. 'My good Mum gave it to me.'

'Your what?' Kate called. Cash and Tessa were a bit ahead, linking.

'My good Mum,' she said. 'My real Mum was a rotter.'

'Where is she?' Kate said, catching up with them.

'Oh somewhere. She's a ballerina.'

'And your father?'

'He comes from dark parts, as you can imagine.' Tessa had a shining dark face, and curly hair, and sharp, no-fool eyes.

'A rotter too,' Tessa said. 'He asked me to go to America and I said to give me time to think about it.'

'Are you going to America, Tessa?' Cash said, worried.

'No, I wrote him a letter. I said, "Dear Father, I cannot go to America with you as I have a very bad cold."'

Without thinking Kate reached out and embraced the strange child, not so much to comfort as to congratulate her.

'Can we have tea?' Cash said, taking advantage of his mother's gust of affection.

They crossed the road to a café.

'Just tea and one cake each, no chips,' Kate said, in case they blackmailed her once they got inside. At the street corner there was a brazier alight, the red cones of anthracite beautifully glowing, and a whiff of heat shedding from it. A man sat by it, half in and half out of a hut. Cash and Tessa stood up, waited for the man to object and when he didn't they then threw the wrapping from the chocolate she'd given them into the fire. The silver ash from the paper lay on top of the glowing red nuts, and they looked on enthralled, their two faces rosy from the light, their gloved hands splayed out before it.

'I have another Mum too,' Cash said, imitating Tessa's voice exactly. 'She lives in my house with my father.'

Kate drew back from the fire, stabbed by what she had heard.

9

Two days later Kate came to meet Eugene at the railway station. It was convenient for him and anywhere suited her. She arrived early and sat in the midst of the chaos, with pigeons tottering around her feet, and people on all sides apparently going or coming to something important. The trains whistled without cease. She went over what she must say to him: that he sack Maura, take Kate herself back and move them into the country to a small white house with a vegetable garden and grazing for two cows. She would grow good, and protective, and cling to him, like the ivy he'd once planted on the gable wall of one of the many houses he'd owned. This figmented house she saw as being in a valley with one huge tree shielding it, so that the leaves got into the gutters, the way they always did. It would be their last home, their stronghold, their coffin. Her mind was made up. It was what she must do.

To ward off the cold and pass the time she got a carton of soup from a machine. After the first sip she looked around for someone to complain to. It couldn't be her imagination, the green soup was washing-up water. Pea plates had been washed in it. She had another sip when it got cool and this verified her suspicions. The dumb blue machine witnessed her protest as she held the carton upside-down so that the soup made an uneventful stream across the tarmac. It eventually settled behind the basket containing orange peel. A man had gone by with a skewer and taken up every piece of orange peel in the place. Toffee papers and cigarette cartons were not impounded, just orange peel. Must be some reason for that. Marmalade? An old, grey, stooped man with his head held down came and cursed her for having thrown the soup away. He had his eyes screwed to the ground for fags and threepenny bits. She apologized, wanted to hand him sixpence but feared that he might curse her more.

'Oh, there you are,' she said, turning. Eugene had stolen up on her. She told him about the washing-up water intending him to laugh, which he didn't. He had leather gloves on and two wool scarves – one around his neck and the other covering the lower part of his face. He kept flapping his hands back and forth under his armpits.

'Are you perished?' she said. She herself was purposely clad in a dark-brown, hairy coat which she'd purchased at a sale. Its dull institutional look might appeal to his conscience.

'It's eight degrees below freezing,' he said. Facts. Facts. Any minute now he'd tell her the strontium content of sherbet. England was screaming with facts and statistics and not one person to supervise soup machines. She moved nearer. He shifted away.

'Well, you wanted to see me?' he said.

'I did.' How to put it, and imply that she was doing it for him as well as for herself? She tried balancing the sentence and out of the corner of her eye saw more orange skin being cast away and at once being lunged at by the skewer.

'It's about Maura,' she said at last.

'Yes,' he said. He had that calculatedly serene voice which

was observing itself say 'yes' calmly, and with understanding.

'I think she's a bad influence for Cash.'

'Oh, and how do you reach that conclusion?'

'His loyalties are at stake. He doesn't know who to love.'

'His loyalties are only at stake if someone questions them.'

'I never question him,' she said in a self-committing burst. 'I never ask if you chat to her, or take her into your study at night. He just tells me.'

'God help us,' he said, over-piously to the roof of sooted glass panels that were backed by steel netting. Her eyes filled with tears. He avoided looking at her. No longer the fixed stare of reproach. He had renounced her in his mind, and through his body. She had always thought that people who had once loved one another kept the faintest trace of it in their being, but not him. He was free of her. Marked of course, but free in a way that she was not. She was still joined by fear, by sexual necessity, by what she knew as love. She tried again.

'It's like a volcano,' she said, 'you and me, it settles down and then it flares up again.'

Whether he thought she was talking gibberish or whether he guessed the implications, he showed no wish to listen.

'You know,' he interrupted, 'the first time I began to fall out of love with you – oh, years and years ago – was the day it hit me like a bomb that you never cry for anyone but yourself.'

'Does anyone?' she said. 'Show me the man or woman who does,' she said and thought to remind him that he had chosen her for his own needs too. His little dictatorship demanded a woman like her – weak, apologetic, agreeable. Self-interest was a common crime.

'Of course. Men have died for other men. Women sweat their youth away.'

What had he done? Talked incessantly about wars, money, injustice, but sat at home stewing in his private pain. And yet he managed to sound superior.

She sobbed, and nodded, and sobbed.

'So that's all you wanted to see me about?'

'More or less,' she said.

He had to be off, he said.

Urgent business. Snow to shovel away from his front path, tea to make and his child to rear. It had become his child. He slipped into the crowd and became one of the many people, apparently going or coming to something important.

A numbness took charge of her brain and she sat somewhere to puzzle things out. She'd missed her chance. It was as if he said he was setting out on a long voyage. How much more comforting if he had just said he was about to die. She knew danger as she had never known it; the danger of being out in the world alone, having lost the girlish appeal that might entice some other man to father her. It wasn't just age; she was branded in a way that other men would spot a mile away, and though still young, she had not the energy to coax, and woo, and feed, and love, and stroke and cosset another man, beginning from the very beginning again. Everything was hazy before her eyes – around her, the heavy flights of the pigeons, and porters pushing trolleys and the drone of tinned music from a loudspeaker. The huge weight of terror that she had been dragging around for years had not lifted on his final exit, but had increased oppressively.

Almost to test this weight she stood up to walk, and bumped into two nuns on the way. Nuns, with their serene faces, and their very white hands lost in big black sleeves. A smell of linen and starch, the black smoking wick of a candle that a nun had quenched with her fingers, the suffocating sweetness of a certain kind of lily. For an instant she remembered her life in the convent, and thought how safe, how wooden, how unscathed she was then. It had all been so long ago. She set herself the task of walking twenty times around a bookstall before she faced the certainty of the future. The icy air cut into her and her feet were damp – snow had melted between the crêpe sole and the upper suede part – but she did not care about the cold. She was panting, and felt that lunatic itch under her armpits as if hordes of crawling lice nested there. A sure sign of terror, for her.

'Walk, walk, walk,' she said. At some point a man went by, with a little girl who had a doll in her arms. The girl was limping.

'Come on, Emily, just a few more steps. Mummy *will* be pleased,' she heard the father say. He had the child by the hand, but at arm's length as if she was a dog.

'I bet you'll eat a big tea, I bet.' They went towards the ticket window and out of some compulsion Kate followed them.

'Will we get a ticket for dolly too? the father asked the child.

'Fuck,' Kate said. Suddenly and unplanned it escaped from her lips and directed itself to his limp, chinless, five-thousand-a-year face. He looked away into the enclosed distance as if he hadn't heard. But he had heard, because he changed his daughter to the other arm so that she would not be corrupted. Kate slung towards a giant weighing machine, and unthinkingly set about weighing herself.

'Eight stone, seven pounds,' a rich, Irish, country accent told her. She talked back to him. There was no question of this being a metal voice.

'Where are you from?' she asked. He was probably shy, thinking she was making fun of him, as no doubt many people did. A grey cloth map on the school wall, long forgotten, rose before her eyes, a map with names that were once names and now which had the intrigue of legion – Coleraine, Ballinasloe and Athy. Ordinary places that she'd never visited and never wanted to visit but were now part of a fable summoned up by this now familiar voice.

'I bet I know,' she said. Still no answer.

'Ever heard of the Silvermines? I'm from there. I didn't go home this Christmas, did you?'

She thought that maybe he had goose with soft, oozy potato stuffing to which sweetbreads had been added. She thought of her father, and wondered why it was that he meant nothing to her at all now. It seemed barbarously unfair that someone could have had such a calamitous effect on her and still not pop up in her mind once or twice a day. Eugene sucked every thought and breath of her waking moments.

'Come on,' she said to the man behind the machine, 'I haven't all day to talk to you.' Although, of course, she had.

She stepped off, took another penny from her purse and weighed herself again. Again he spoke. He was still there.

'I bet you find Sundays in London lonely,' she said. 'I bet you miss not going out in the fields with a couple of hounds and a gun.' A thing Irishmen loved to do.

'Please,' she said softly, 'talk.' She tapped the glass, waited, to hear his breath first, then the voice saying, 'Hello,' or,

'Where do you come from?' the way these voices greeted one in dance-halls.

Possibly twenty seconds went by. Then something broke loose inside her and she started to scream and bang the glass that covered the numbered face. She hurled insults at it and poured into it all the thoughts that had been in her brain for months. She lashed out with words and with her fists and heard glass break, and people run, and say urgent things. She was held down by the shoeshine man until the ambulance came, and she came to, back to reality that is, in the casualty department of a large hospital. At first she only stared at the bandages on her hands as she heard the soft-soled shoes of nurses walking by on the rubber floor. Then she remembered, first one thing, and then another, how he had come, how he had gone, she threaded their conversation together, then recalled what she had said to the man with the child, then the weighing machine, then her heart beating madly before the outburst of violence. Every detail was crammed into a capsule, so small and tight, and contained, that she would carry it with her for ever.

A nurse asked if she was all right and if they could telephone her husband to come for her. They'd seen her marriage ring. She said no, that he was gone on a voyage but that she had a friend that would come. They let her telephone from the almoner's office and a nurse stood over her while she did it. She got through to Baba.

'Cut out the opera-star stuff and get over here,' Baba said, when Kate explained the predicament.

'You're waiting in for me, oh bless you.' She had to say that, in case she would not be released. More outrage from Baba.

'I'll be there in half an hour,' she said and hung up, telling the nurse that her friend was expecting her and everything would be all right. To her there was something disastrous about losing grip on oneself, like a dead woman she'd seen once on the road with her clothes above her knees and one shoe a bog of blood. On her way out, she got a card to come back in a day or two for a check-up. She went into the cold street, panting because her strength had been drained away. It was a narrow escape.

10

Well, curiosity killed the cat and information made her fat. That little salubrious interlude with the drummer had its results. In other words the months went by and I did not have my regular visitor and could not eat a breakfast. I began to wonder, what could I do? When did it remotely resemble a child, because what I had to do ought to be done before that? I was musing over this in my tobacco-toned room, listening to the Swedish bitch banging the vacuum cleaner all over the house when the telephone rang. As you might expect I had to sack Cooney the minute I got the wind up. She'd be following me into the bathroom to watch me being sick. I said we were going to Rome for a year. I didn't care what I said.

It was Brady from some hospital. She'd had a little argument with a weighing machine at Waterloo Station and took this to be the end of the world.

'Get over here,' I said, 'there's a real kicking problem.' And I said it so furiously that she did.

First of all I had to get rid of the Swedish bitch.

'How about takin' the afternoon off, hah? Nice shoopping and buoy friend,' I said.

'Goood,' she said and dropped the Hoover without even turning off the switch. She was off in no time, wearing one of those marvellous-looking Norwegian jerseys that would make any man think she was good-looking. Kate arrived soon after with her face of woe. Guess what she talked about? Them. He didn't love her. She'd met him. His words were brutal, final and meaningful. She *did* love him, but sometimes she didn't. The break came in a bus, when she was all dressed up in about nine petticoats and raging that they had to bus it. She said to him, 'If you sat on the other seat I'd have more room,' and he took this to be significant, and so did she, and that was how the break came.

'Shut up,' I said. I couldn't take any more of that. Garbage.

'There's a real live problem facing us, get your thinking cap on,' I told her.

'What?' said she.

'The old, old story,' I said, sort of singing it, to make it less awful.

'Love,' she said. If you say potato famine she'll say love.

'Preg.,' I said, remembering that I'd said it to her before when we were in Dublin and she'd said, 'How?' and I'd said, 'The usual way,' and she'd said something else, and I'd said it was easier than owning two coats. Well, the conversation repeated itself, verbatim. At least this time we had money and we had drink, and she didn't know it but I had a gallon tin of castor oil in the shed, if the worst really came to the worst.

'But children are nice,' she said. 'You're fond of Cash.'

'It helps,' I said, because she may have got a scholarship, but in some ways she's a moron, 'if they have a trace of their father's eyes, ears, nose, feet or something. Would I be that frantic if it was orthodox?'

It dawned on her. She wanted to know who. What was he like? What was it like? Did I see him often? Was I in

104

love? Should we go and see him? See him! He'd belted to Greece! I was in two minds whether I should tell her or not that it was all her fault. But the thought of a big ream of apology stopped me. It was action we needed.

You won't believe it but she asked me was I hoping it would be a boy or a girl.

'Twins,' I said. 'Two of each.'

She got all soppy then about irony, telling me a card she'd seen in a 'For Sale' window which said: 'Unworn maternity dress, fine grey check, seen any time.'

'Poor creature,' I said. 'We'll go around now and buy it.' I gave her a look that would cut her. Then I armed her with three crisp pound notes and sent her out to buy a medical book so we'd get all the dope. (I'm beginning to talk like my mother.) Anyhow she came back hours later with a big dictionary that cost five pounds – she had to expend two of her own – and it has to be seen to be believed, this dictionary. It said things like: 'Catarrh, disease of the nostrils.'

'Get the preg. data,' I said, because she's brighter than me in educational matters. She began to read about Fallopian tubes and raised her head from the printed page to tell me she knew a woman who had two and having two meant you could have two children by two different men at the same time. I was enjoying this, I really was. I took the book out of her hand and looked up under A for Abortion. They didn't even consider that word.

'We'll have to get a doctor,' she said. 'Some nice understanding doctor.'

I couldn't go to the shark down the road that I usually went to, because he's our family doctor and a Catholic. We got the telephone book and rang specialists. I'd have paid seventy-five quid, for God's sake. Well, they had it all so fixed that you had to have appointments made *before* you were pregnant – like booking for that Eton lark when the babies are conceived, before they know whether they'll be cretins or not – and you had to have a letter from your family doctor. We thought of friends. She knew someone who knew someone that had a friend who was a gynaecologist. About ten phone calls ensued and the final one was me talking to this hag who was a lady gynaecologist in the Knightsbridge region. She had one of those voices you hear in second-class hotels where people are pretending they don't know it's a second-class hotel.

'Fur example,' she said, 'aur you bleeding alort?'

'I wish I was,' I said. She got very dodgy then and found that her appointment book was full for an indeterminate time.

'I hope your vowels move tomorrow,' I said and rang off.

'What now?' said Kate, fatalistic. If I hadn't been in such a mess I'd have said she was sick and ought to be in bed.

'You ought to know someone,' I said, 'with all your connexions'; with her Madame Bovary slop I thought she'd be adequate to it. 'Or even a crook who'd do a job on a kitchen table in Bayswater,' I said. She gave off a big spiff. How these crooks live a lurid life and make a fortune by telling about it in the Sunday papers. She said they had little typists living in terror.

'They can go to hell, they won't get my money,' I said in a fit of sympathy for those goddam typists whoever they are.

We went back to the dictionary.

'There's people all over London, happy at this moment, and people getting on buses, and doing normal things,' she said.

'I'll swap them this house and all this gear for it,' I said. We were really low. She had a grey coat on that you could sieve vegetables through, and her skin was dry like an old cooked potato. Her eyes, that used to be her good point, were gone back in her head from crying.

'I'll buy you a coat,' I said.

'Did you marry him for money?' she said. I said I didn't know.

'Do you hate him?' she said. I didn't know that either.

'I don't hate him, I don't love him, I put up with him and he puts up with me,' and then I thought of this new disaster and how it would kill his pride and I got frantic again.

'Baba,' she said, 'once you have the child, it will be all right. You'll both find it is the most important thing in the world to you. A woman needs children. I'd have more myself.'

'Right,' said I, 'we'll go on a world cruise for our nerves and come back and say 'tis yours.'

Boy, did she change her tune. She wasn't ready for children, she said. Who is?

I knew then that it was up to me and I'd better do something, so I told her about the bath and castor-oil plot and asked would she stay, in case I got drowned or had a heart attack. I know she'd really like to have run but she stayed. I'll say that for her. Not that she was much use. She nearly fainted three times, what with the steam, and the greasy look of the castor oil in the cup, and me sweating and moaning and retching. I had her play 'Careless Love' on the record player. She had to go out and put the needle back on that part of the record each time that it changed to another song. I thought it was kind of apt.

Suddenly I turn round in my sweating condition and she's kneeling down with her hands joined.

'Get up,' I said. 'Get up, you lunatic.'

'I'm praying,' she said. She hadn't said a prayer for years and even I thought it a bit steep that she should be asking help of someone she'd ignored for so long.

'Nothing short of sacrilege,' said I, knowing that would put the wind up her. She was on her feet like lightning, and off to change the needle and put more coal in the boiler. I could hear that boiler roaring up the chimney and I prayed it wouldn't burst or anything until this ordeal was over. He'd kill us. I had cramp and pains and I began to shake all over. The whole place looked weird. The mirror was all fogged up, and steam all over the place so that I couldn't see my own make-up and stuff on the various glass racks. I'd look at the hot tap running, then all around, then directly down at the water hoping to see its colour change, then back to the tap again and all around and I don't know how long I did that.

'Kate, Kate,' I said, holding on to the bath as if I was sinking.

'Kate, Kate,' I yelled and roared, and she came and said I'd better get out.

'Are you out of your mind?' I said. Imagine going through all the pain and sweat and sickness that I'd gone through and then give up in the middle. I was shaking like a leaf and she held me.

'Good old Florence Nightingale, little old lady with the castor oil,' I kept saying, so that she wouldn't think I'd gone too far and call a doctor or do something criminal.

'Jesus,' I said suddenly, because it was like as if I was stabbed in the butt of my back. I began to howl.

'I'll get brandy,' she said.

'Don't leave me, don't leave me,' I said. I was dead certain that if she left me I'd fade out. Anyhow she let go my arms and I just lolled there and next thing I know she's giving me brandy from a spoon and saying, 'I'm going to phone Frank.'

Frank! That revived me. I came to for long enough to say, 'If you phone Frank I'll take twenty-four sleeping pills right now.' She gave me more brandy and turned off the hot tap. I knew as she was turning it off that my chances were over but I hadn't the energy to resist. The steam, the heat, the castor oil and then the drink had made me feel like straw. She swears that when I passed out a few seconds later I was a hefty weight to haul out of the bath.

I came to in my own bed with two dressing-gowns on me. The first thing I did was to see if anything had resulted because I'd had a feverish dream that I was in a train and it came, and I couldn't get off the seat and porters were standing over me yelling at me to get up. Only in the dream had it come.

'Hullo, little old lady with the castor oil,' I said to her, sitting there. 'T.D.L.,' I said, because I was damned if I was going to get all morbid again. No man was worth it.

'Total dead loss,' she repeated after me. She was more grave than me.

'We'll get our minks on and hitchhike to the Olympic Games,' I said. 'I'll enter for the egg-and-spoon race.'

She didn't laugh. It was about four o'clock on a lousy afternoon in March but at least the house was warm because of the way we got the boiler whizzing.

'The gardener came,' she said. I could hear him shovelling the snow away. All he could do that winter was shovel snow away so that we could get our Jags in and out, and get up the front steps, drunk, without falling. Not that I'd have minded a fall at that time. It was grey and awful looking and I got her to put on the light and draw our sun-drenched blinds.

'Well, it's now for some crook,' I said, and pitied those typists again. I was sorry for everyone and no one, the way you are when you're in a mess.

'You can't,' she said.

'I go to crooks to have my hair washed,' I said. 'Where's the difference?'

'The difference is that one is just frivolous, and the other is violence.'

Well, Christ, I roared out laughing. I mean think of being in the state I was, and someone going on like that. Then she launched into a sermon. A whole lot of highfaluting speech about how I was trying to destroy myself, murder part of myself. A parable, just like the way it was in the Gospels. They'd all eat fish and then sit around and hear a story.

Hers was about some woman who was having a baby by a man who loved her, and she didn't want the baby. So she got rid of it. The man stopped loving her, and she fell madly in love with him and went around with a terrible loss in her, because she'd killed two good things.

'But it's not Frank's,' I said. As if she didn't know.

'But the point is,' she said, 'that you don't know beforehand what damage you do to yourself by your actions. You only know afterwards.'

Well, I couldn't dispute that. I proved it every ten minutes of every day.

'You know her too,' she said.

'What is she like?' said I. There was something about

that story that gripped me. I knew I'd be looking out for that woman in the hairdressers.

'We're going to tell Frank,' she said, 'when he comes in this evening.'

'NO.' I didn't want to tell her the bit about him getting berserk when he got angry. If we told him there wouldn't be a stick of stuff left in the house and nothing of me, only bones.

'He'll wreck the joint,' I said.

'We'll go to his office,' she said. 'He can't wreck anything there.'

'NO,' I said.

'Look,' she said. She was off again. Another sermon.

The upshot is I'm dressing myself. She's telling me to put on white make-up and no lipstick and to look wretched. It is not difficult. She'd got me into such a state of right- eousness that I was ready to be a suffragette for ten minutes. She said we wouldn't take a car, no, we'd go in all humbleness by bus or Tube. It was miles away in North London. I can tell you I was pretty wobbly from what was behind me, and from what lay ahead. We damped the boiler, put on our coats and set out.

Down in the Underground there was a gas advertise- ment. It said, 'Do nothing until you've read *Vogue.*' Well, in our plight, and with people starving, and having pyorrhoea, and all sorts of things I thought it was very vital advice.

'We must come down the Tube oftener,' I said.

'I come every day,' she said, making me feel like a rat.

Then a great big enormous pregnant woman appeared from some archway and that was enough to make me run for the exit stairs.

111

'Come back, come back,' Kate said, catching me by the belt of my camel coat. That minute a Tube tore into the station and she linked me into a 'No Smoking' compartment. We changed into the next compartment at the next station and had a fag each.

'We'll have a few gins along the way,' I said. Even she was beginning to lose her fervour.

We got there around four. That was the first time I'd ever been near any of the building sites. They were putting up new blocks of offices on a bomb site and the ground was snow and yellowish muck. There was an arrow underneath a home-done sign that said 'Inquiries at office', and we went in that direction; men booed and whistled at us. Such commotion, such noise: hammers clattering and hammering, a great bloody bulldozer churning up more yellow earth, a drill whining and men on the scaffolds yelling in Cockney at Irishmen underneath who couldn't understand a word they were saying. A din. I prayed that the brother wouldn't be with Frank.

'Don't apologize,' said Kate, knowing that it was her own worst trait.

'I might funk it in the very middle,' I said.

We found him alone in a small, fuggy, little corrugated-iron office with plans and papers laid out all over the table in front of him. He was on the phone.

'Christ,' he said, when we came in without knocking.

'No, no, Lady Constantine,' he said into the phone, 'it's just that somebody's capsized a bottle of ink over my notes. ...'

It was about a cesspool that he was going to install in her country cottage. We got bits of the conversation. While she was talking he put his hand over the mouthpiece and said like a savage to Kate, 'I hope we haven't to get you out of another mess.'

I was kind of glad that I was going to shatter him.

'Yes, it has its own waste-disposal system,' he was telling Lady Con, and I knew it was about this cedar-shingled place he'd put up for her in the country. She started on about the roof then. The slates must have been cracking and spalling all over the place. He got red in the face and raised his voice.

'The roof!' he said. 'That roof was perfect.'

Next thing he was apologizing for his language and saying, 'I'll come down there myself.'

God help the roof, I thought. He could do a good thousand pounds' worth of damage in five minutes.

'At no cost to you,' he said. Then he told her not to worry, and that his bark was worse than his bite. Finally and after a typical jarvey-drivers' farewell he put the telephone down. Kate stood on my toe just to give me a bit of courage. He didn't look at us for a minute, he wrote some big important nothing into his desk diary and sat there frowning at what he'd written. I could not believe that he was my husband and that I sometimes slept near him and had seen him sick and drunk and in all sorts of conditions. He was another man in that outfit.

'We haven't come about me,' said Kate, quite indignant. 'We've come to tell you something.'

'You'd better make it snappy,' he said, 'the men knock off at five and we have our conference.' He called the men together every evening, and the big, brutal foreman of a brother told who was slacking during the day. Just like the countries we read about where it's supposed to be coercive.

'You tell him,' Kate turned to me.

'You begin it,' I said.

'It's yours, Baba,' she said, very stern. In the end I had to.

'I'm going to have a baby,' I said. He grinned, a terrible pathetic grin. It was like telling someone his mother was dead and you beginning the sentence and he getting it all wrong and thinking his mother had won money. For a minute he thought it was his and that he'd proved himself. He stood up to kiss me but I put my hand out straight away. He went like a block of wood; he stayed quite motionless in that position which is half-way between sitting and standing and he didn't utter a word. The telephone rang.

'Will I answer it?' I said. He picked it up and threw it and I ducked, knowing the throwing craze was on. He got more fluent than he'd ever been in his whole life.

'You cow, he said. 'There's a way to deal with you and whores like you. I'll kick the arse off you when I get you home.'

'I'll take a boat for somewhere,' I said.

'You'll do no such thing. You'll bloody well stay where you are and do what you're told.'

'Did you think I was going to live frustrated?' I said, just the posh way Kate would say it. I could see he didn't understand that word. There's lots of words like frustrate and masturbate that he doesn't understand.

'It's not very much for a woman living the way we live,' I said. 'All that huntin' and shootin' and fishin' lark is all very well in company,' I said. He began to close his fist and turn his bottom lip outwards the way he does when he's furious. All this thing about women and new freedom. There isn't a man alive wouldn't kill any woman the minute she draws attention to his defects.

'Watch your language,' he said. Boy, it was hot in that room with a double-bar electric heater going full blast.

'I can leave you,' I said. 'I don't care about a scandal.'

He knew of course that it would cause a setback between him and the bishops, and be bad for his work too because a lot of the big contracts he got were from big Catholic firms.

'I'll tell you what to do,' he said.

I could hear heavy footsteps outside crushing their way along the cindered path and I knew that help was arriving. It was the brother to say the meeting was due in a couple of minutes.

'Tell your brother,' I said. 'He's a great one in a crisis.'

The brother killed someone in Ireland once and drove on but was found. They would have jailed him except that he bought his way out.

'Get out,' he said, knowing damn well what I meant.

'When I get home there won't be much of you left,' he said.

'I won't be there,' I said and wrote the telephone number of Kate's dump on a piece of paper, so that he could ring me if he wanted to.

'What's up?' the brother asked. He has a murderously red face and curly hair.

'The stork,' I said as brazen as hell. My knees may have been wobbling under me but I kept a good front up.

We muddled our way through the muck and got on to the road.

'The eyes of workmen are permanently screwed up, they have to keep them like that in case mortar flies into them,' she said. I thought it a boring piece of data, but it got us out of there to the dark street, to bus queues of people.

'Oh no,' she said, suddenly defeated. Lucky I had money and could get a taxi to her dump.

'I'll be shacking up with you,' I said. 'You needn't be lonely any more.'

She looked worried. She's all unnatural about babies and birth.

He rang me about ten. He'd cooled off considerably. He said:

'I've decided to let you stay on as my wife – in theory only, of course.' Nothing new about that.

'That's great,' I said. I suppose he expected a great slob scene from me about how generous and charitable he was. Not me. I know the minute you apologize to people they kill you. Then he wanted to know whose it was so that he could go around and kill him.

'He's a Greek,' said I, 'and he's gone home.'

It was the only thing I could think of. Kate had her head out the bedroom door. She was as inquisitive as hell.

'Will it be white?' said he. The eejit doesn't know Greeks from Blacks.

'It might,' said I, 'if we're lucky.' He said he wanted no more cheek from now on and I had to do what I was told and nobody was ever to know the truth.

'Does Brady know?' he said. He hated her.

'Of course,' I said.

'Keep her away from the house. Pay her to keep her bloody mouth shut,' he said.

'And go to Confession,' he said. He then told me he was having a much-deserved holiday to get over the shock and if anything urgent in the business line arose I was to telephone the secretary.

'Have a nice time,' I said, and dashed in to Brady to tell her she could live in elegance with me for a week until he got back.

'It's an ill wind,' I said, and she finished the sentence, 'that doesn't blow good for someone.'

We laughed. A thing we hadn't done for ages.

I was in the bathroom trying to change things around – since our misadventure the very sight of it depressed me – when lo, Durack appeared. It shook me. He hadn't shaved for the three days since I last saw him, and he smelt of booze.

'You're still here, arsing about,' he said.

'Where ought I be, in the Magdalene laundry?' I said, whistling like a man.

'That'll do now,' he said. He stood in the doorway, he was nearly the width of it. He took a bit of a blonde lady's hair out of his pocket, it was in the shape of a ringlet.

'Recommend her to your gentleman friend,' he said. 'Wonder worker.'

'You recommend her,' I said, 'you're the authority.' I reckoned he was telling me he'd been to some brothel and got a testimonial and I was mighty glad.

'I find I like it,' he said, 'vicarious living.' Well that was a new word for certain.

'Insertion at various angles,' and he looked at me, quite drunk. 'You get my drift?' he said.

'It's made a new man of you,' I said. I suppose he thought I ought to show jealousy or temper, I showed nothing. I was quaking.

Then he began to curse and swear in a blackguardly way. Such a volley of language. Unparliamentary. Words we never parsed at school. Then something checked the words on his tongue as if there was another him inside the blackguardly part, and he started to cry and I said for God's sake to hit me, assault me, kill me, do whatever he had to do but to get it over. I took a step forward. He looked at me, big child's tears on his face.

'Isn't it a fact that I gave you everything you want?'

'It's common knowledge,' I said. That worked terrific. Instantaneous. Remorse. He began to cry harder but it was collapse and not temper that invoked the tears.

'Baba, why did you do it to me?' he said. Useless to say that I hadn't thought of him when I was doing it. Useless to say that I always thought your acquaintanceship with one person had nothing to do with another. Or to say all the things that went on in my head, the longings, for songs, cigarettes, dark bars, telegrams, cactuses, combs in your hair, the circus, nights out, life. He wouldn't understand.

'I was drunk.' How could he but forgive that condition.

'It was in Hyde Park,' I said. A man's home is his castle.

The way I said it he could see it was no great event and a bit of spunk came back into his voice.

'Like dogs,' he said. I thought 'Not even like dogs,' but I sang dumb. I thought how I had this daft notion that men could make you feel it all over, and make you half faint at the same time, and it was a mystery to me where I picked it up from.

We heard Brady let herself in and heard Cash call our two names and I for one was glad of their arrival. She brought the kid for high tea and I told him this.

'She knows?' he said.

'She's demented, she knows nothing,' I said. He was glad of that.

Then he came right in and closed the door and began to talk in whispers. He said he'd give me a second chance but on conditions. Never, never was I to do it again or he'd slay me alive.

'I'll satisfy you,' he said. Ah, the land of promise. It was quite a pathetic thing to hear him say, his eyes down. I reckoned he was feeling pretty terrible. Then he caught hold of my hand and said we were never to bring it up again. We were to keep it a dark secret. Poor devil, he told no one, not even the brother. So the big Biblical bond between them was all my-eye. They were allies in nothing only making money. When it came down to fundamentals, he had no one. All by himself and that brothel he went to. There was just us, him and me. Allies, conspirers, liars together. I took the line of least resistance. In the eyes of the world it would be his and mine. I said O.K. What else was there to do? Among other things I didn't relish going out into the world to sell buns or be a shorthand typist. It would have his name.

'Give me your word,' he said. I blessed myself. The visible sign of the cross. Salvage began. We shook hands and went out. Not very light-hearted of course but then how could it be otherwise.

Our family doctor arranged for me to go and see a gynae-cologist and I went one boring afternoon when lots of other people were sitting down to tea and shop buns. The nurse that let me in had very thick glasses and her eyes were teary behind them. Not that it mattered. I wasn't feeling very sympathetic. He asked me how long I'd been married and were we delighted to start a family. I had to say yes, of course. They were all Catholics. He asked me how I felt, and I told the bit about cooking Brussels sprouts in the middle of the night, and having bile in the mornings. He asked me a ream of questions about whether I'd had miscarriages, tummy-aches and other morbid ailments. I'm the kind that gets these complaints if someone reminds me of them. He wrote it all down, dead serious. God only knows how many lies I told.

Then he sent me to another room and told me to pass water. I didn't know whether I'd be able to pass water or not – it isn't a thing you can do to order. I went up there anyhow and had a look around. There was a lavatory and wash basin with a pair of yellow rubber gloves on the side of the basin. They were sprinkled with a talcum powder that smelt of babies. I'd forgotten that smell. There was a picture that was supposed to be a joke. It was a crazy drawing and the caption said that before you have a baby you ought to measure the size of your husband's head. As I heard him coming up the stairs I mounted the black leather couch that had stirrups at the side. I knew that they were to put my heels into for the examining bit and I was hoping to God that I wouldn't make a fool of myself.

He came in real casual. He asked if I backed horses. He began a long rigmarole about how he'd nearly brought off a Tote double. All this time he was easing the rubber glove on to his hand and then smoothing it out so that there was not a crinkle in any of the fingers. He told me to grip my heels in the stirrups and I never felt so helpless or so obscene in my whole life. Just prostrate and facing a window as well.

'I would have won quite a penny,' he said.

'Waterlogged?' he said. Humour!

'You're trying to be funny,' I said.

'Relax,' he said, sort of bullying then. Relax! I was thinking of women and all they have to put up with, not just washing napkins or not being able to be high-court judges, but all this. All this poking and probing and hurt. And not only when they go to doctors but when they go to bed as brides with the men that love them. Oh, God, who does not exist, you hate women, otherwise you'd have made them different. And Jesus, who snubbed your mother, you hate them more. Roaming around all that time with a bunch of men, fishing; and sermons-on-the-mount. Abandoning women. I thought of all the women who had it, and didn't even know when the big moment was, and others saying their rosary with the beads held over the side of the bed, and others saying, 'Stop, stop, you dirty old dog,' and others yelling desperately to be jacked right up to their middles, and it often leading to nothing, and them getting up out of bed and riding a poor door knob and kissing the wooden face of a door and urging with foul language, then crying, wiping the knob, and it all adding up to nothing either.

'All right?' he said. I took deep breaths.

'I wish,' said I to him, 'that I'd been born a savage.' So I did, where women aren't tightened up, and just drop the babies out of themselves and go on cutting sugar cane or whatever the hell savage women do.

'What an extraordinary statement,' he said and I could feel his finger withdrawing. More pain, more pressure. I wondered if he ever got fresh, or if all that disinfectant and stuff put him right off. He said yes indeed that I'd started a baby. He put it in a way that nearly made me sick.

'God has fructified your womb.' That is the exact way he said it. Then he said how pleased my husband would be and he talked all sorts of technical stuff that I didn't want to hear. All about embryo.

He went down ahead of me while I retrieved my knickers from my handbag and put them back on.

Downstairs he got the runny-eyed nurse to write out for me when I was to come again, and he gave me a prescription for iron and vitamins. All I wanted was a prescription for ergot, or whatever it is wise women take. I came out and sat in the square opposite, where it said 'Residents only', and I cried bucketfuls to the tune of 'I came. I didn't think I would.' If only it had been Durack's. Don't ask me to say crime does not pay because I'll say it, but I'll also say virtue does not pay, it is all pure fluke, and our lives prove it. Kids, I thought. God help them, they don't know the bastards they're born from.

11

The silence was shocking. Even the clock on his desk did not tick though it gave the correct time. Kate looked around: the rubber plant was still there and the couch with the sheet over it. Did other patients lie down? Some of those nameless, awed people who sat outside in the waiting-room, the ticking shadows, preparing to spill out their woes. He gave them pills each week – tiny white pills packed into tiny circular boxes – and fifteen minutes of solace. It allowed them to keep numb, get on and off buses, walk the dog, and go to bed at night without being tempted to carry a pillow downstairs and bury their heads in the hire-purchased gas oven. It enabled them to die slowly.

It was Kate's fourth visit to the psychiatrist and she found she had nothing to say, or had so much that it was useless to cramp it into the time allotted and then stop and retain it until the next week. Desperateness by instalment. She was looking at this pale, thin-lipped man who sat like a dummy and had heard her woes as if he was hearing the weather forecast. After the Waterloo debacle Baba's family doctor decided that Kate should see a psychiatrist because she was unstable. He'd sent her to the outpatients' department of the local hospital. On the first day she'd done nothing but weep, and on the second she'd talked about

Eugene and of how she'd given him false proportions – set him up, as one sets up things that are past. Like thinking that the weather was always fine when one was young, and that the hedges were full of wild strawberries, when, in fact, there were only a few hot days, and the strawberries were hearsay, found by Baba or said to have been found. Anyhow she resented telling about her marriage. It not only violated her sense of privacy it left her empty. Life after all was a secret with the self. The more one gave out the less there remained for the centre – that centre which she coveted for herself, and recognized instantly in others. Even vegetables had it, the very heart of, say, a cherry, where the true worth and flavour lay. Some of course were flawed or hollow in there. Many, in fact. Was he? This spruce Englishman in his pink shirt with the collar held down by pill-white buttons. She would have to sleep with him to know. The only way of ever really knowing a man. The thought sickened her.

Before she left Eugene she had often thought of being with other men – strange distant men who would beckon to her, and as she moved they would draw back their coats on their naked bodies, and have her float away on the wing of the wavering out-thrust penis. Mostly dark-horse men. But one was blond and had pale-green eyes like the whey of the milk. But now that she could taste the mystery of other men she declined, and shrank back into her dream.

'What are you thinking?' the psychiatrist asked. Half the allotted time gone.

'Of a plane crash,' she said, cheating beautifully. The words came out of nowhere.

'One you escaped from?'

'No, I read about it. One hundred and four people were killed outside Boston or somewhere, and when the cause of the crash was investigated afterwards by millions of experts, I mean by experts, they found the engine went wrong because starlings had nested in it. That haunts me.'

'Why?'

'Because I feel like the starlings.'

'You feel you kill people.'

'I feel I sort of destroy them, with weakness.'

'How many people have you destroyed?'

'I do not know,' she said, and began to sob suddenly and uncontrollably. He offered her a tissue from the box on the desk, probably kept there to accommodate the numerous cryings that went on.

'Come on now, pull yourself together.' The old cliché. She sat hunched, staring down at the damp, disintegrating tissue, struggling to control herself. Why had she said such a thing? Why had it upset her? She longed for him to comfort her. She could not bear to be seen crying by someone who wouldn't for that duration enfold her, the way hills enfold a valley. Hills brought a sudden thought of her mother and she felt the first flash of dislike she had ever experienced for that dead, over-worked woman. Her mother's kindness and her mother's accidental drowning had always given her a mantle of perfection. Kate's love had been unchanged and everlasting like the wax flowers under domes which would have been on her grave if she'd had one. Now suddenly she saw that woman in a different light. A self-appointed martyr. A blackmailer. Stitching the cord back on. Smothering her one child in loathsome, sponge-soft, pamper love. She tried to dry her eyes only to find them re-leaking. She stood up, made another appointment with the psychiatrist, and went through the waiting-room so distraught that she wrung the pity of people who were worse off than herself.

At the bus queue she cried more, and in the bus she kept her head fixed to the window-pane so that when the lady conductor came she handed her sixpence although it was only a fourpenny fare. Simpler. For days she went around hating her mother, remembering her very minutest fault, even to the way her mother's accent changed when they visited people, and how after going to the lavatory in some strange house or some strange hotel she would make a feeble, dishonest attempt at washing her hands, by putting one hand – the one she'd used – under the tap, when at home she just held her legs apart over the sewerage outside the back door, where they also strained potatoes and calf meal. In that fever of hate and shame she thought one day of something that lessened her rancour. They had laughed together once, and Kate put great premium now on laughter. It happened when she was eight or nine. She had gone with her mother to collect three dozen day-old chickens from a Protestant woman who lived near the graveyard. They took the upper road because it was shorter, but it was more tiring to walk on, not being tarred.

'I want to do a pooley,' her mother said. 'Watch for me.' Her mother never took time to do a thing, hardly ever sat on the lavatory and consequently had piles. They looked up and down and then the mother squatted, just around the bend. Kate, the child, wandered off a few yards and began to daydream, as she always did out of doors with birds and tall blades of sighing grass to make her fanciful. She was thinking of the day she bought a stamp and held it by its sticky side on the very tip of her thumb, and the wind which made the grass sigh swept the twopenny stamp away.

'There's a man, a man,' she said suddenly, running to where her mother squatted. He was cycling downhill at a terrible speed.

'Where?' her mother said, stepping on to the middle of the road with her navy, nunnish, gusset-reinforced knickers down around her legs. The brown river she'd made was coursing over the dusty road finding its inevitable destination to settle and be dried by sun. It was summer-time. The sun was bleaching the green, ungathered swaths of hay.

'This way,' the child said because her mother looked in the opposite direction. He came round the corner and prised through the mother's parted legs with the front tyre of his bicycle. They both fell and were locked by the handlebars.

'Sweet Jesus, I'm killed,' the mother screamed.

'No, but I am,' he said, as he tried to extract himself from the bar and from the woman.

'Where in the name of God were you going?' she said as she put her hand on the dusty road to ease herself up.

'I'm going to a funeral,' he said, taking up his bicycle and shaking it fiercely to make it straight again. He wiped the saddle with the lining of his raincoat and swore under his breath. The chickens that had been left on the grass bank were screeching through their perforated box and the child had hidden her face in an enormous dock leaf.

'You ought to look where you're going,' the mother said, walking towards the chickens with as much dignity as she could muster. As she walked she tried to ease the knickers above her skirt.

'The same goes for yourself,' he said as he speeded the bicycle forward, ran with it, put his leg over the bar and cycled off saying, 'Townspeople.'

'Ignorant yahoo,' the mother said when he'd gone. She

rested against the grass bank then, and laughed at the scratches on her hand, her grazed knee, her ripped knickers, the idiotic saddle of his bicycle stuck up in the air like a dog's nozzle.

'Going to a funeral,' the mother would say, and they would laugh, and double up, and remembering some other moment of it they would start a fresh bout of laughter.

'My good knickers at that,' the mother said. Everything was funny.

But they were never able to talk about it again because the mother got shy once she had laughed her fill.

Ah, childhood, Kate thought, the rain, the grass, the lake of pee over the loose stones, the palm of her hand green from a sweating penny that the Protestant woman had given her. Childhood, when one was at the mercy of everything but did not know it.

She did not go back to the psychiatrist the following week. Her excuse to herself was that she had to find some place to live. Cousins, friends, in-laws, some of the nameless stock people that come to the rescue on such occasions were on their way to take her room. They were announced by the landlady the morning after Kate was caught having Cash in the house. Eugene had given permission for him to stay with her, one night. She bought a chamber-pot and warned Cash about not going out on the landing. Once in bed he wanted the game – the old one in which she became a ghost and frightened him.

'Go out, and come in and be a ghost,' he said.

'We can't play it, you know that.'

'Because of the old grump.' He knew a little about the landlady with the pasted-on smile and the snarling, asthmatic dog.

'Well, go behind the curtain,' he said, 'and be a ghost.'

She did, and no sooner had they begun the game than he begged to be tickled and frightened into insane laughter. There was a knock on the door, and the landlady barging in, discovered the child in his pyjamas, in bed. Kate said she could explain everything but the landlady saw it as a piece of treachery. Kate took him home early next morning.

'Tell me about the First World War, how many infantry there was,' he asked. She couldn't tell him. She didn't know. 'Chew your gum,' she said. She'd bribed him with four gum balls from a machine because that morning when she forced his feet into his socks he'd said, 'When are you coming home for ever?'

'I don't know about the First World War,' she said, 'I wasn't born.'

'Well, the Second World War,' he said.

'I don't know about that either,' she said. He made a wronged face and resigned himself to counting all the toy-shops on his side of the street, which the bus passed by, and told her to do the same.

In the afternoon she began to look for a bed-sitting room. She knocked on doors, spoke clearly, swore that she was white, house-trained, had no pets, could dry her clothes magically in a hay-box and would keep her radio (a thing she didn't own) to a mute whisper. And to the three who thought of considering her as a lodger she suddenly excused herself on the plea that she must think about it. She ran from their terms. She ran to another address. There must be a Bowery somewhere.

In the end she found a small, single-storey house in a terrace of identical houses. They looked like drawings out of a child's story book, small and dark with tiny turret windows and a stone cherub over each door. Inside it was so dilapidated that Baba said it would be a cinch for entertaining the bicycle-chain, orange-box set.

They went to an auction room and bought the necessities.

'Where's my smelling salts?' the pregnant Baba said, advancing sideways up the narrow passage between the mountains of used goods. Kate felt disgust. A smell of homes that were, stained mattresses, mildewed, bed ends on which hands had laid the pickings from their noses; sofas farted into, the dregs of lives. Baba bid – a table, chairs, one armchair, a bed, a wardrobe and an umbrella holder. On the way home they bought a tin of disinfectant and a spray gun, just to be on the safe side.

'We'll fumigate it,' Baba said, trying out the empty spray gun in the hardware shop. They also bought new ash-white wooden spoons, and a fish lifter, and a kettle, and a chemical to make the sink sweet-smelling.

'You'll need this,' the man in the hardware shop said, holding up a white shell.

'What is it?'

'A water softener.'

'We'll have it,' Kate said. There was something ridiculous about everything she did. Homes were not put together roughly, like this.

Baba blessed the house with a bottle of whisky and they drank while they waited for the men to deliver the stuff.

'There's no doubt,' Baba said, looking around at the job-lot wallpaper, 'but you've got on in life, Katie. You've made a good match.'

The wallpaper was purple with red veins on it, like a graph of someone's lousy blood-stream. The same pattern throughout the house.

'This will be a real salon yet,' she said as they sat in front of the fireplace nursing rubber hot-water bottles.

The slight eerie noise of soot falling through the chimney and rustling on to the crêpe paper, which had been laid into the grate, got on their nerves. The fire could not be lit until the chimney was cleaned, and the chimney could not be cleaned until the electricity was turned on, and the electricity could not be turned on until the wiring was repaired. Broken sockets fell away from the wainscotting, and where they had already fallen off wires stuck out like two evil eyes of danger.

By the time Cash came the furniture was installed and the Victorian armchair was held up partly by books and partly by castors. He sat on it. He too thought it was a house out of a story, where a witch might live. But he was excited.

'Good, good,' he said, marching around the rooms, stamping on the boarded floor, rejoicing because everything was so empty and therefore free to wreck.

'I must go, Katie, or I'll get murdered,' Baba said. The place bored her. If there was one thing she couldn't stand it was bare boards. These particular boards were the limit altogether because the previous owners had let their kids daub them with every colour paint under the sun.

'I wish you could stay,' Kate said, seeing her to the door reluctantly.

The sky was green and watery. Kate said it would rain. Not just rain, Baba said, but thunder and lightning and deluge and floods. She also said to remove the 'No hawkers, no circulars' sign from the wooden gate because hawkers wouldn't waste their time coming near the place. The path was strewn with leaves, papers, and rainwashed notes to the milkman that had blown in from other porchways. The wall between her and her neighbour was too low. She'd put trees there so they wouldn't have to talk. Talk would only lead to questions, and then condolences and then friendship. She had no energy left for friendships.

Cash tried pulling off the sign with his nails and then with a fork, but it was firmly screwed on, and the screws had rusted into the metal sign.

'Come, we'll go around the house and plan what we'll put in all the rooms,' Kate said. He'd shed a few tears when Baba went.

A Turkey carpet here, a brass fender there, a picture of soldiers for Cash to look at, geraniums, a new pink bath, a lavatory with china flowers in the bowl, occasional tables, and woolly rugs that he could snuggle into when he took off his shoes to have a pillow fight.

There were green spots of damp on the four ceilings, and older fainter stains like rivulets running from these damp spots across the centre of two ceilings. A big roof job.

'Can we have bunk beds?' Cash said. He was hitting the walls and floors with the new wooden spoons, making bangs.

'Bunk beds!' she said. She was making up the secondhand bed in the front room where they would sleep together that night. She put the hot-water bottles in, and lit the paraffin heater. It was brand new; its wick white and unblemished.

'Now what do you vote we have for tea?' she asked. It was essential to keep busy and to keep him busy because of the awful emptiness. Rashers and beans on toast. They ate off their laps, in the front room, close to the heater. Cash liked it better than a table because when the beans skeetered off his plate he could reach down and pick them up.

'You'll be able to bring some of your toys here and leave them here,' she said, wanting him to settle in.

'Can I have new rockets?' he said. 'And when will we have a telly?' She thought how pathetic that she should have to win him back with goods.

The evening stretched on interminably. It was still only six o'clock and they had finished tea, washed up, put the chemical in the sink and gone around the house, laying a candle in a saucer in each room, with matches beside the saucer, in case they needed to go in to any of these rooms urgently, in the middle of the night. She'd brought one red candle as a celebration and put it in a scooped-out turnip on the mantelshelf. She was telling him about Christmas when she was a child, and how they'd always had a candle in a turnip on the window-sill in case Christ went by. He'd never seen the place where she was born. He knew nothing of the weeping, cut-stone house where all her troubles began. And he had no interest in the boring story about being afraid if her mother went upstairs to make the beds, and eventually having to follow her mother up. He wanted to draw. There were no pencils or papers. They searched the two wall cupboards and found only damp, and one shrivelled football boot.

'Draw on the window,' Kate said. 'Be resourceful.' It was thick with grime outside and dust inside. A yellow street light had just come on and cast light on the two dirty encrusted window-panes. Later in the evening, before they got into bed, she would have to hang a sheet or something, because the street gaped in at them. Later still she would have to buy material, and measure the windows and make curtains, and hang them up and draw them in the evenings to shut out the gaping street. There would be the noise of curtain rings running back along the rods, and the fire flames leaping on the wall and people sitting down to eat. What people?

She looked across to see if he had done a house, or a pussy cat, and when she saw the enormous 'HELP' daubed across the sooty pane she put her hand to her mouth and gasped. It was when she ran to console him that he must have become aware of something catastrophic happening to him, because suddenly he began to cry in a way that she had never seen him cry.

'I want Dada,' he said.

'We'll get him,' she said.

'Now,' he said.

'What's the matter?' she said. 'Why are you crying?'

He wanted paper, pencils, television, toys, warmth, bunk beds, things he knew.

'Look,' she said, sitting him on the bed and pushing back his fringe so that his very creamy forehead showed. She kissed its cool creamy texture and told him how forgetful she was not to have all these things, and promised she would have them next day. He did not like the candlelight either. 'It might turn into something else,' he said. It was fitful and it threatened to go out when the wind blew down the chimney. She pressed him in her arms, to give him shelter, and to revive the solidity that had gone out of their lives.

'I want Dada,' he said, sobbing in her embrace. He smelt of cool basins of cream in a pantry at night. When she first carried him his feet pressed against her stomach, and later on he bit her nipple with impatience, but at no time had she felt so close to him as now.

'I'll take you home,' she said, rising. The tears which seemed to have been overflowing from him vanished as if he'd put them back in his eyes, as into a reservoir.

In the taxi he kept looking out of the window, commenting on the darkness. He could not face her, he felt too contrite.

'I'll come back if you want me to,' he said, and when she did not answer he said, 'Mama,' but very softly, and very tentatively, as if he feared he had failed her.

'You'll come back,' she said, 'when the electricity is in, and things are cheerful.' He had reminded her more than she'd ever known of the terror of being young, of that fearful state when one knows that the strange, creepy things in the hallway are waiting to get one.

'I thought he wouldn't care for it,' his father said, jubilant as he met them at the door. Maura waited somewhere behind, and Cash went in the house calling her name.

Late that night it rained. The first, harsh swift drops rushed through the garden tree and down the outside of the window, inside which she'd hung the patched sheet. It was one she had pinched from Eugene's cupboard one day when collecting Cash. But Maura saw her do it so she didn't have a chance to take any more. Maura didn't like her. She knew from what Cash said. They had been passing a linen shop and Cash saw pillow-slips for elevenpence.

'We'll get some for Mother,' he had said.

'No, we won't, we'll get them for Father,' Maura had said. It told everything.

The sudden sound of rain startled her. She'd been sitting for hours listening to sounds and up to then she'd heard footsteps outside, passing along, and voices passing along with them, the flurry of soot falling, and the letter-box flapping as if someone or something from the outside world was coming through. But it was wind. She wanted to go to the lavatory but couldn't. Terror had gripped her. It began hours earlier as a knot in her chest, and it went down to the pit of her stomach and now it paralysed the tops of her legs, enveloping them in cages of iron. She could not move. Some awful thing waited outside the door for her. By morning she would be crippled. The strange thing was that the monster outside the door would only harm her if she went out. It would not come in. She jumped up and opened the door, asking it to show its face, but saw only the dark of the hall which she didn't know sufficiently to locate what recess it had stepped into. She closed the door again and came back to her seat, knowing it was fruitless to scream because nobody could come to her rescue. But terror has its own resources, and when she climbed through the front window she had no idea she was so distraught. Her neighbour, who had come out to put a tarpaulin over a scooter, turned and said, 'Are you locked out, love?'

'No. Locked in,' Kate said. She realized it was funny a second after saying it. The neighbour – a fat woman in an overall – straddled the low wall and came to help.

'You're at sixes and sevens,' she said, looking into the front room. Nothing to her own place which was a little palace. She'd have a whisky, and love to. They climbed in. She told Kate to see that the milkman kept his hands to himself and not to forget that bins were collected on Tuesdays and always to knock on the wall if she wanted anything. After she'd sympathized a bit about moving in winter she got down to her own troubles. How her man had upped and left her one fine day and now she was afraid of her life he'd come back because she was happier by herself. She had a boy-friend of course, but men were different when you lived with them. She also said that for a young person Kate had a very startled face, and that the house could be improved and that it was a dreadful night but gardens benefited and never to underrate the pleasure of gardens, flowers, trees and plants. She left when Kate had calmed down. At least the terror had passed away and she smiled when the woman said 'If you're interested in ballroom we might make up a foursome.'

'I might be,' Kate said, chagrined by her numerous inadequacies. At least it is true she was trying to smile, and she had not mentioned the child, not once. The woman, staggering a little from whisky, was about to get over the wall but on second thoughts decided to use the gateway and walked with ridiculous dignity.

12

Early summer days. The garden which had been so savagely empty in winter began to reveal things: lupins, dog-daisies and some wild kind of rambling roses that fell apart when they were touched by wind, or the clothes from the line. Although it was May there was still frost, and some mornings the clumps of thistles were a sight to see. Erect, knife-edged, covered in silver. Six months now. Spinster days and untrespassed spinster nights, except for lying awake and dreams. She often dreamt that they were back together, and in the dream she welcomed it, but not in real life, when she saw him she acted cold, wary, indifferent. Jealousy had passed away. She spotted them from a bus and Cash said 'Look, look, Dada, Dada.' It was late evening and he was driving across a common in his car that was itself the colour of dusk. It could be Maura, or then again it could be somebody new but she had no wish to know. Would that they drove to the horizon and right out of the world, leaving her and Cash to their own devices. A war was brewing. They'd stopped meeting because he wrote and said it afforded him no pleasure to gaze upon her destroyed face and her mean little dagger eyes. She thought his stares carried more hatred than her own, but knew she was not a perfect judge. They were each plotting, separately but

thoroughly, both assuming total injury, both framing ugli-
nesses that would tear to shreds the last, threadbare
remnant of their once 'good' life. It was for Cash, they said.
But what is a child between injured parents? Only a weapon.

He had found someone and so must she. But the effort!

'You could bloody well trick someone into thinking you're
swinging,' Baba would say, over and over again.

'I don't want to,' Kate said. And didn't, until one specially
lambent summer evening when her new telephone gave out
a shrill and totally alarming ring. No one knew her number
except Baba and Eugene. But this was a woman's voice, a
total stranger asking for Kate. It turned out to be a pho-
tographer who'd once photographed Cash.

'Hiding away like a little old mole,' she was saying. 'Had
to get your number from directory inquiries.'

'How are you?' Kate said. She hardly knew the woman.
They had met in a coffee shop. The woman liked Cash's face
and asked to photograph him for an exhibition she was
holding. Like everyone else, she said at the end of the session
that they must meet again. She said she lived with a madman
who did papier-mâché figures and that Kate would love him.

'I'm ghastly. He cracked my skull and I have double vision.
Oh yes, he's still here, absolutely,' she was now saying.

That was the unnerving thing. Other men and other
women survived their mutual slaughterings. She compared
everyone's behaviour with Eugene's.

'When is it?' Kate asked. The woman had rung to ask her
to a party. The word 'party' still had evocations, like the
word 'myrrh', or 'Eucharist', or 'rose-water', or 'pearl-
barley'.

'Now, this very evening,' the voice said. 'And you've got
to come.'

Why not. Not quite ready for a second flowering but conscious of that all the same. A summer evening. And all her clothes beautifully clean like clothes waiting for an outing. Since she worked in the cleaners' she had everything pristine all the time. It also happened to be the night on which she did not have Cash. She and Eugene had him on alternate nights and either one took him to school next day. He was a schoolboy now with a life of his own, and a desk, and picture books and crayons that he had to be responsible for. One day she went to look at his homework, and in one of those copy books she had read a composition which he'd written; and for which he had been given a gold, paper star. It was entitled 'My Life' and it said:

I live in a large cave with my mother and father. Each morning my father goes out hunting, if he is lucky he catches a deer. While he is out my mother dusts the cave.

'I'll come,' Kate said, and took down the address. She dressed herself in blue (Mary, star of the heavens) and put on blue beads that 'like a rosary' reached down to her navel.

Outside the evening had a sort of golden afterglow that held the world in its thrall. Gold-lit houses, slant in Thames water. Little boats going by silently, silent men pushing their way unambitiously with the help of a single oar. The tide was high, the river water clean and solid, giving the illusion that it could be trod on, as if a silvered swaying roadway.

She walked for a while, conscious of how gay people were, of how many bright pairs of red jeans were abroad, and how many birds. She'd forgotten that birds sang!

The key was in the door and noise streaming down the stairs conducted her accurately to the room filled with people and many, many candles in gilt bottles. She paused for a minute at the threshold, apprehensive: meeting a roomful of people was not the same thing as thinking about them when one is on one's way and bus windows are a fiery gold. They had drawn the hand-weave curtains and shut out the evening. The music was so loud that she could not identify any face; once her hearing was impaired, she also seemed to stop seeing. Bad coordination. A man, some man, in an open-necked shirt came over and greeted her.

'You've just arrived and you look lost in that beautiful dress and your name is what and what do you do?'

She asked if he were the papier-mâché man, and when he said no she felt no obligation to be courteous, so she heard herself say that mainly she got through. He let out a rich, congested laugh and begged her to tell him more.

She went away from him towards the drink table, towards her hostess who was wearing gold lamé to match the bottles that contained the candles.

'Darling, you look different. What happened?' the voice, somewhat husky, projected to her. She laughed it off and accepted a whisky. After all the hostess had had a cracked skull. Possibly everyone in the room had had a catastrophe, so why should hers be condolable?

'Darling, just make yourself known to everyone,' the hostess said. Kate looked around. Two coloured men were arguing. Sophistication. She thought of telling them of a sign she'd seen in the Underground which said 'Nigs get off our women', but they might not laugh. They might just tell her to hoof off. There was a time when she could have approached anyone. He noticed and came across, the same man who first greeted her. His name was Roger. Jokingly he began to strangle her with her own necklace.

'You're a bit fresh,' she said, thankful all the same. He was very good-looking and that worried her. For months now she'd been spouting to Baba about the accident of physical attraction. She'd even decided that she would never have fallen in love with Eugene if it weren't for his sepulchral face.

'I am aloof,' he said. 'Except when I meet a very beautiful woman.' He was so affected he may even have been real.

He was alone obviously, because no woman's eye trailed him, as women's eyes do, in the most crowded and ill-lit rooms. He was standing much too close to her – hip to hip, you could say.

'Listen,' she said, faking indifference. The woman was telling another to ring Daphne, because Daphne knew where to get antiques for nothing, and Daphne's lavatory was trad., and Daphne knew scores of handsome, potent, unattached men.

'I wouldn't think you need Daphne,' he said.

'I could do with antiques,' she said, picturing her four rooms, two of which were empty except for tea-chests and the folds of paper in the fireplace on to which the soot dropped. She was on the verge of telling him about it when he said, 'You're married?' She still wore the plain gold that she'd bought for herself anyhow, because Eugene didn't believe in outward proof.

'Yes,' she said. Then a girl came up behind him and chained his neck with thin, tanned arms and locked hands. Kate went off. She made herself promise that she would not cling to anyone, or confide in anyone, that she would skim through the party, coming and going like the soft gold moths that

came in the window, fluttered about, and went out again.
Except that some made straight for the candle flames!

In the kitchen there was food. Clear soup simmered in a
vat. It reminded her of the soup she'd once had at Waterloo
Station, but she helped herself to a mug all the same. Perhaps
some sane person would come and talk to her.

'It's the greatest,' a small Scotsman was telling another
small Scotsman, with witnesses standing by. They all wrote
plays or sonnets or toothpaste ads, they all had something
self-important to say.

'Are you an Irish nurse, or an Irish barmaid, or an Irish
whore?' some kind goat-bearded man asked her.

She acted as if she was a deaf mute and that too made
them laugh.

More people came in, smelling the soup and the steam,
mistaking the laughter for real, calling each other by familiar names: Do and Jill and 'Issa, the shortened names that
were for longer names but whose use made people feel they
would never be quite so alone again.

'He has the old falsies et cetera,' one joker was saying of
a man who posed as a woman. The story had cachet because
the poseur was a television actor.

'My hair grows an inch every day. I sit up in bed watching
it grow,' a starlet type said. The same one that had put her
arms around Roger. She was nibbling the ends of her buff-
coloured hair, waiting for someone to tell her how pro-
vocative it was.

'When Clarissa is hungry she just eats her hair,' Roger
said dutifully. A yes-man.

'Yes,' said Kate with weary humour, turning to Clarissa
but meaning it for him, 'if you were in a chorus you would
be almost certain to make the front row.'

How bitchy she had grown! She moved away, apparently warming her hands on the mug of soup that was already going cold.

In the next room they were dancing and she slunk in there and found a stool. She'd picked up a drink on the way and drank it with the soup. In the small dark room the carpet had been rolled back and the floor was cramped with people who shook, and wobbled, and looped their arms, and lolled their crazed and craving heads. Sometimes and for a brief moment, in the pause as one record followed upon another, the various partners came together, and the woman simpered, and the man took hold of her crotch, putting his claim on her, the way he might spit into his drink before going to the Gents in a public bar. One man asked a redhead if her hair was the same colour down there.

'Come on, doll, you're not swinging.' A tall man stood over Kate. She looked up and shook her head slowly from side to side, a thing she learnt once, to relax her neck muscles.

'I'm drinking,' she said.

'You're not swinging,' he said. He had a ruddy, affectionate face and golden eyelashes. She would have liked to talk to him. She would have liked to say, 'I can't dance. I drink instead of dancing, or I cry.' She would have liked to say, 'Teach me to dance,' or, 'How many of these people sleep together?' but he was exercising his shoulders and flicking his fingers to the beat of the very loud music.

'You won't,' he said. 'You're not a primitive?'

'Later,' she said. He moved on to the floor and joined a girl who had begun to dance alone, in defiance. She was tall, and boyish-looking, and wore leather trousers.

Sitting, watching very carefully, Kate tried to do the dance mentally. She shook her arms, her legs, her hips, her shoulders, but she could not trust herself to stand up and do it.

'What do you think of it?' the papier-mâché man called over to her.

'Great, great,' she said. The password. He was dancing with a girl who wore a strawberry punnet on her head to make herself taller. He winked at Kate's sandals. They were toeless and silver, with straps as thin as a mouse-tail across her instep. She held his look idly for a second and then she looked around to locate another drink. She poured some from the stray glass into her own, and drank it greedily. If nothing else, she'd get drunk! There were now two record players and two opposing songs were belting out; the faces of the dancers were twisted with effort and mistrust, the sweat crying on their brows. It was hot, and unfunny, and shrill in that room. And a little tipsy, Kate thought what the coolest thing she'd ever known had been: the exhalation of fresh brown clay; that inaudible breath when the sod is first turned over.

It was a habit of hers to escape a bad moment by remembering a better one. She thought of a day when she said to Eugene, as he walked naked across the bedroom floor, that a man's testicles had the delicacy of newly forming grapes. It must have been summer, both because he was able to wander around naked without freezing, and because the sight of hanging grapes was fresh in her mind. Far away and lost all those moments. Part of her had died in them.

'Come on, I'm having an erection, let's go,' the papier-mâché man said to the girl with the strawberry punnet and they both shot through the door. Kate followed, stunned. She had to see if they were boasting.

They were not in the bedroom at any rate. The large

145

double bed was piled high with coats and to one side of the bed, lying in its crib, was a baby looking up at the ceiling with the deepest, darkest eyes. Eyes that only babies have, that are like powdered ink when the first drops of water have been added and it is still an impenetrable blue. The baby hung a lip and thought to cry when Kate's form mooned over it, but being resourceful Kate remembered a game from Cash's infancy. She ducked behind a bank of coats, reappeared, and went on ducking and reappearing until the baby's giggles alerted other people. Its mother came and tapped a pillow just to show she was its mother, and Roger came, and stood near Kate, and said, 'You must be a very real person.'

'I am,' she said. 'I help blind men across the road,' as she gave her finger, out of some buried instinct, to the child to gnaw.

'Auch,' she said, taking it away quickly, and to him, 'Trust not the innocent, this child bit me.' He opened his mouth and snapped quickly at nothing, as if an apple had been swinging from the ceiling on a thread. He admired her cheek-bones. He asked why she hadn't danced and why she looked on with such scorn. He had been watching through the jamb of the door. She wanted to tell him the truth, to say that she felt clumsy, and tired, and considerably older than twenty-five, but she heard herself saying something quite different.

'They scream too much and they perform too much and they have no cadence,' she said. She was really drunk now, using words that were affected and trying to sound superior. He asked what she'd been thinking of.

'I was thinking of clay.'

She could not have said a more propitious thing: he saw

her now as fundamental. Where had she come from?

'Ireland,' she said. 'The west of Ireland.' But did not give any echo of the swamp fields, the dun treeless bogs, the dead deserted miles of country with a grey ruin on the horizon: the places from which she derived her sense of doom.

'There is a solitary stone castle,' she said, as if she owned it, 'on a hill and it is intact, even down to the beautiful stone window frames, and there is always a white horse there, rooted to a cleft of the hill, and I would like to live there.'

Lies. Lies. He fell for it, he said he must go, *they* must go there, make a pilgrimage, ride the white horses over the bogs down to the churning sea. She had filled in some details for him to be able to describe the place back to her.

'Sssh, ssh,' Kate said and put her finger to his lips. The baby's eyes were closing. She had forgotten that terrible anxiety which grips one in the instant that a baby is going to sleep, in case it won't. She remembered Cash and felt disloyal to him. Then she put a scarf on the side of the crib to shut out the glare of the table light, and looked up, smirking. She'd forgotten the pleasure of watching a man become attracted to her.

'You've made the party worthwhile,' he said.

'And what about the others?' she said, meaning the soft, the bunny, the gooey, the dew-wet bitches.

'They are all lovely,' he said. Rat. She'd expected some corny little lie at least.

'I must go soon,' she said to her cheap wristwatch, as if it would save her. A woman who had just come to get her coat was having an argument with about twenty other coats, which she pitched on to the floor.

'Find me my bloody coat and take me home,' she said to Roger. Did she know him? Maybe not. That was how people paired off now. Many met for the first time, lying down on a bed that was bound to be unfamiliar to one or other of them. Kate shuddered, longing to be safe, in a taxi driving towards her own house.

'But I have a girl,' Roger said, introducing Kate.

'Have two,' the woman said bluntly. 'You're a man, aren't you?' He repeated that Kate was his and turned to her to confirm it. Will-less now, a little drunk, trapped, she let his hand caress her stomach in a slow, circular motion.

On the way out he excused himself for a minute. To say good-bye, or make a date for later with the drunk woman, or pinch a bottle? What matter.

They drove in the opposite direction to where she lived. She wanted him to say something, to ask him where they were going and what he intended to do. Sometimes he took his hands off the wheel and flicked his fingers and wriggled his shoulders as if he were dancing to impress the wheel. He had put the radio on.

'Careful,' she said. She always thought of Cash in moments of danger.

'I'm never careful, I pursue death,' he said.

She kept one hand on the dashboard just in case.

They drove to a road named after a plant, where his flat was.

'I'll remember this road,' she said. The mildness and the warmth of the evening still touched her with remaindered joy and she put out her hands to catch something.

She wished that they could walk. Walk and walk and delay it, or maybe avoid it. It was a luxury now to walk at night, because she had no man to escort her. No placid male friend.

'You are rare,' he said, 'and beautiful, and I want you.'

She hadn't quite faced the sleeping question. She both expected it and didn't. She was not certain what to do. Did other people make love in the same way or were there bed secrets that she didn't know about? To have only been with one man was quite a drawback. They climbed tall steps to the door, then climbed a staircase and another and another. His room was an attic with a door cut out of floorboards. He wound a pulley and the floor lifted up and she climbed a few more steps and entered a room that was large and cluttered, with two enormous windows at either end, facing each other. He had clicked on the light and picked some clothes off an armchair to make a seat for her. The door came down slowly, filling the gap in the floor, and finally closing with a slight thud. It was not unlike being in prison. Evermore when she thought of the word party she would think of the wilful internment that came after.

'You're cold, all of a sudden,' he said. She sat on the bed very close to him and they drank vodka from tooth-mugs. A white cat with a hump on its back sat surveying them.

'I want you,' he said and bit at her the way he had bitten at an imaginary apple before remarking on her cheek-bones.

'Wronged eyes,' he said, 'big too.'

'Sometimes big, sometimes small, depends on how tired,' she said, and stood up. To keep indifferent, to keep cool, to keep her heart frozen. In the mess she was in now anyone could take advantage of her. She'd trade anything for scraps of love.

In the bathroom there were three different colours of eyeshadow in small, circular boxes. Three different sets of eyes had looked in the split mirror and drank from those Cornish tooth-mugs and sat very close to him on the bed. Also a copper ring, on a twig. Things left behind by people who were certain that they were coming back. The door between the bathroom and the bedroom was missing. How was she going to use the lavatory when the need came? From the bed he waved in to her. 'Hello,' he said. Then when she came out he went in there and the telephone rang. She picked it up but no one answered.

'Leave it,' he said. He stood at the lavatory for a few minutes and she could see his dark form and his hand, palm downwards, on the wall.

'I can't do it,' he said. So he was as shy of her as she was of him. Relieved, she crossed over and held his hand and they both waited and prayed for that pee the way people wait in the drought for rain. She said she liked the smell of fresh pee; it was when it got stale that it got sordid. She said did he notice when he ate beetroot how red it became.

'Never ate beetroot, only rhubarb,' he said. He said rhubarb backwards for her. They said it together a few times and then he did the pee, and just when they were about to sit and celebrate the telephone rang again.

'It must be Donald,' he said.

'Who is Donald?' she said, disbelieving before she even heard.

'Donald is a dear sick man whom I must go and see,' he said.

'When?'

'Now. Tonight. I promised him.'

'I'll come,' she said.

'No you won't. You'll wait here.' He held her shoulders, said she mustn't behave like a child, that she must get into bed and sleep, and then waken up fresh when he got back. He lit a cigar, aimed the red glow at one of her eyes and put on the suede jacket which he'd taken off when they got in.

He licked his finger and placed it prayer-wise on her pulse. A little baptism.

'Wait there,' he said. She was certain he was going to another woman. He wound the pulley up again and went down the stairs, raising his forehead on the last step to signal up to her, and then the door closed again and became part of the floor, and this time it was really prison. The humped cat looked at her, the night appeared beyond the two windows that were at opposite ends of the room. An aeroplane went by, its green lights passing over on a level with her eyes. She ought to get down the stairs before it fell on her head and knocked her out. She ought to and she could. The cat never stirred. She dreaded having to stay only a little less than she dreaded having to go. And so she stayed. The beggar. There were books all around she could read or she could rummage and find little inklings of his life, but she just sat there staring across the room towards the window where she'd seen an aeroplane go by. 'I've come to a nice end,' she said aloud, and thought where are convent scruples now? He hadn't forced her, she'd come of her own accord to get a little – what? Satisfaction probably. No use ennobling it. Simple case of physical famine. In the end she took off her shoes, her stockings, her roll-on and put them behind the leather sofa where they would not catch his eye, and after about an hour she took off her blue dress, and got in between the sheets that were spattered with dried white paint.

When he got back she was dozing.

'I'm still here,' she said, sitting up, hiding her face with her hands, apologizing.

'Sssh, ssh, back to sleep,' he said and undressed, and slipped in quietly beside her. Nothing happened for a few minutes. She put her hand in his and squeezed it over-tight. How dreadful if he rejected her now. How indecent. He seemed cold, temperate. Perhaps he'd gone and ... She closed her eyes ashamed, unable to finish the thought.

'Would you prefer to sleep first?' she said. That stung him. He moved up and lay on her, with dead-weight. The pet words, the long, loving handstrokes, the incredible secret declarations that were for her the forerunners of love-making, all these were missing. Pure routine. The way he might turn on a fire extinguisher in a public building if someone called, 'Fire, fire.'

'You don't really want me to make love to you,' he said. His way of saying that *he* didn't. She watched his interest in her fade as she had watched others fade before now. The 'instant love' potion proving useless once again.

She ran the soles of her feet up and down the calves of his legs, increasing the speed as she went along coaxing herself into a fake frenzy. She remembered all the times she had longed to be with a man, and she told herself that she'd better make the most of this, it might have to see her through yet a winter.

'You want orgasm,' he said, cruelly. She'd heard that homosexuals, who, out of deceit or vanity, forced themselves to sleep with women, inflicted these sort of humiliations. She simply shook her head and smiled. Vulgarity, indifference, lovelessness – these things did not surprise her any more. She had wanted orgasm but all she wished now was that they could extract themselves without losing face.

'Don't analyse us,' she said, kissing his shoulder and coyly admiring its costly tan. Sweet Jesus, she thought, I despise him. If there was a way of making him suffer now, I would do it. If he said his wife had vanished with his babies I would smother my last grain of pity and laugh. It was the first heartless admission she'd ever made to herself. The first time she realized that her interest in people was generated solely by her needs, and bitterly she thought of the little girl, herself, who had once cried when a workman stuck a pitchfork through his foot. It was as if her finding the pleasures in the world had made her ravenous.

'All the women I've loved still love me,' he said.

'Many?' she said, to humour him.

'Many,' he boasted, dwelling on the word as if they were passing through his mind in a procession; lovely still-headed women.

'Any particular age-group?'

'Young,' he said.

And he had been the one to say to her at that crowded party, 'What is absent from your life I must give to you,' and she had been the one to swoon.

She stroked his back, asked where he got the tan, moved her face from left to right, smiled, frowned, made little jokes, all to let him think that she did this sort of thing often and was not a fool in a strange bed. She thought of a pencil sign she saw in a pub lavatory which said 'I married Charles six days ago and I haven't been fucked yet', and how its cruelty had shocked her, just as her own cruelty was shocking her now. With desperation she began hugging him, pressing her nails into his back, begging for kisses. She who had come home with him in heat was dry now and quite systematic! Out of decency she would have to arouse him and feign delirium when the time came. What a cheat. Especially when one had set out to get something for oneself.

Afterwards he said he should have waited longer but she

hushed that, and uttered something predictably noble about first-time hazards.

'I'm going to sleep,' she said, 'and I'll want tea when I wake up.' She could be quite flippant after all.

'Are you talking about tomorrow?' he said.

'I don't believe in it,' she said. But earlier that night when he first flattered her she had had some wild notion that he might fall in love, heal her, provide new thoughts, new happiness, banish the old ugly images of fresh-spattered blood, and forceps, and blunder, do away with Eugene, the guardian ghost, who shadowed her no matter what streets she crossed or what iniquitous sheets she slipped between. She honestly believed that this man, or some man, was going to do all this for her. Ah! He was going to sleep now, turning over to face the window that faced the sky where the aeroplane had gone by, hours and years ago. She curled up, accommodating her body to fit into the hollow of his. She thought how nice if women could become the ribs they once were, before God created Eve. How gentle, how calm, how unheated, how dignified, to be simply a rib! She pounded the pillow to get rid of some knotted flock and whispered, 'Good night.' Then she drew the sheet up over her face and closed her eyes.

But it did not work. She could not sleep because of the strangeness, and as the night wore on she dreaded the morning. She dreaded sitting up and having to say 'Hello' and watch his thoughts curve away from her the way a river changes course when it encounters a boulder. He already said he had to go out early. He already hinted. She moved to the foot of the bed and got out, without even touching the hump where his feet were. She dressed carefully, studied the door mechanism and then lifted it up, creeping away without a sound. She left no note. Another narrow escape.

Out in the street the stars, if there had been any, had vanished and the light was deepening from dun-grey to a tenuous satin blue; blue light touching the slates of the high houses, approaching windows, behind which people slept and had made love or had dreamed of having made love or had turned over to avoid the face and breath of some hated bed-companion. People were strange and unfathomable. As well as being desperate. He would be relieved to find her gone.

In the Underground station she counted her money and rubbed the tops of her bare arms. The Tube rushed like wind into the empty station and she stepped into a 'No Smoking' compartment along with two other girls. Had they come from illicit beds too? They were well organized: they wore eyeshadow and had cardigans and carried small travel bags. If the day got warm they would remove their cardigans and put them on again in the evening. She closed her eyes; they had already closed theirs. She closed her eyes on the thought that sleeping with a man was unimportant. A nothing, if nothing in the way of love preceded it. Or resulted from it. Did these girls know this? If the Tube was about to crash and they had seconds' warning what was the last thing she would cry out? This new-found knowledge, or Cash's name, or an Act of Perfect Contrition? Impossible to tell. Anyhow they were getting there safely, only three stops to go.

At work she rang him. At least he was a man. He might introduce her to someone else and that someone ... Even in sober unslept daylight she hankered after the De-Luxe Love Affair.

'You are not a one-night girl, you are for all time,' he said, rambling on about how easy it would be for him to fall in love with her.

'I just wanted to apologize,' she said and dragged in the plea about having had too much to drink.

'I would have liked to make you happy.' He was solemn now.

'But you did make me happy,' she said hurriedly, rushing in with fake assurances.

'When I get back from Budapest we must meet,' he said. The writing was clear on the wall.

'Have a good time there,' she said. Just as well. He probably knew that any man she took up with now would only pay in pain for what had happened between her and Eugene; the brutal logic of wronged lovers taking their revenge on innocents and outsiders.

She put the telephone down and for the couple of minutes that remained until opening time she stood facing, but not looking at, the 'ticker-tape' sign of multicoloured lettering which at that moment was still but would soon be flashing on and off guaranteeing bargains, perfection and total satisfaction.

The fierce arid clarity that comes from sleeplessness possessed her. She foresaw the day: four hours there, the awful smell of cleaning fluids, the stupidity of dirty, crumpled clothing, the panic on the faces of people who had lost their dockets, then relief at identifying their own garments; she would have a two-and-ninepenny lunch, her daily walk by the Thames, possibly the tide going out abandoning old shoes – why always single shoes? – and pieces of soggy wood and men's contraceptives, pigeons grey and black and white pecking for nourishment from the relegated semen on the muddy tideless shore; and at four collecting Cash from school and taking him to a playground to swing the swings and home to tea. Another night. But not for long. The time was coming, and she could feel it almost like music in her bones, when things would be different. It would be better once Baba's son could talk and walk. He would be a brother for Cash. Michael, Baba had named him, or rather it had been Frank's choice. In the end Frank received him like his own and made even greater consequence of being a parent than if he had actually been one. And Baba, never one to be held down by punishment, was cornered in the end by niceness, weakness, dependence. Still she and Baba would take a holiday, for a week or two they would live as they pleased, tell fluent lies, have love affairs, dance at night, learn to ski, and slide down mountain slopes, temporarily happy with their children. She had no place in mind, but they would find a place. Baba would attend to that because Frank no longer restricted her in little things. Quite often he was too drunk to register. He merely waved an arm and said, 'Powerful, powerful,' to whatever was going on. There would be some very good days, weeks perhaps. And smiling at the thought she saw the ticker-tape move and heard the grunt that machines give before they start up and knew that downstairs the manager had turned on the switch that set the day in motion.

But it did not turn out like that at all. When she got to the school gate Cash was not waiting. No surprise. He was invariably last, or arrived in his school plimsolls and passed her by, forgetting that it was the day to go to her house and not his father's. When he did not come she went to the cloakroom in search of him. All the metal hangers, but one, were free of coats and the place looked alarmingly forlorn without either coats or children. The blue anorak hanging there belonged to a much older child. She called. She then stood outside the lavatory and called again. She remembered some drama about his being locked in the lavatory by an older boy and she called now very loudly so that he could not fail to hear her. In the end she went to the headmaster's door and knocked nervously. He received her in a small neat office where he sat before a cold cup of tea.

'I can't find Cash,' she said.

'I'm sorry, the school is sorry ...' he said with a shake of the head and added 'Mrs ...' simply to acknowledge her married status. He obviously did not know how to tell her so he asked her to sit down.

'I wasn't sure if you knew,' he said then, lifting the cold cup of tea and handing it across to her. He told her how Cash's father had come and announced his decision to take the boy away. She was seized with giddiness and once again obliged to ask herself if she were not perhaps dreaming or sleep-walking.

'When?' she asked. For a minute she believed there was some connexion between her wayward night and the father's decision.

'Last Friday,' the teacher said.

Five days before. So there was no connexion. This seemed to give her strength. She seemed to recover her senses and drew herself up in order to rise to her feet and then some invincible and implacable force possessed her whole body as she rushed out of the office and down the corridor and along the five streets to his father's house.

When she hit the knocker there was no answer and she knew there would be none and yet she repeated the move again and again and pressed the disconnected bell and peered through windows that were coated completely with white chalk. Once she had seen them through snow and now through another snow she was looking and seeing nothing. It was a big moment, the one when reality caught up with nightmare, the crest and the end.

Next day there was a short letter from his solicitor enclosing a longer one from him. And both these letters told her everything she had screamed to know when she clawed the door, rapped her knuckles on the windows and pleaded through a fastened letter-box to be heard, to be answered. They had fled. Cash, Eugene and Maura. A flight into Fiji. She could see now how it had been carefully and beautifully worked out, as careful as a major robbery. He saw to it that she got no inkling until they had gone, and it was this that drove her to the last pitch of desperation, this mindlessness of hers. How little had she observed him. She still thought that perhaps she could catch them out, that perhaps they had broken the law.

She rang the passport office and after frantic explanation to a telephonist and then a secretary she was put through to the official who had in fact issued a passport for Cash. She asked why she hadn't been consulted and the clerk said that a mother's signature was not necessary for such a thing.

'You call that just?' she said.

'What?' the man at the other end asked.

'Oh, balls,' she said savagely and hung up. The conspiracy was too enormous, the whole machinery too thorough, it was like seeing a newspaper heading that read 'Holiday Coach Crashes' and experiencing a senseless futile blinding rage.

Eugene's letter was long and self-righteous. He said he had lost a daughter through a woman's heinousness and he was not going to lose a son. He outlined her faults, did it so thoroughly, so intelligently, that half the time she found herself nodding, agreeing with him, the words scratched out with care, with cruelty, indisputable, final words – 'Vain, immoral, mean-minded, hard-hearted, weak, self-destructive, unmaternal.' She skipped and read further down. 'There is no other course open to me than to carry out my duty as his father to the bitter end. I will not allow you to destroy his future life, to turn him into one of those mother-smothered, emotionally sick people, your favourite kind. What infection, it can hardly be called thinking, makes you take for granted your well-being as of paramount importance over that of the boy's healthy future, over my work and life. It is too late. You should have planned your full-time mother career a little earlier when he was being reared by Maura and myself.'

Too late! She cried out, 'You are mad, mad. It is all mad, senseless.' One idea after another suggested itself and these were not very far removed from madness either. She would go there, set fire to the house and rescue Cash, she would have the boy stolen from school, no she would beg, appeal to his tenderness, send a telegram saying 'I carried him, I bore him,' blackmail them, get a letter from her old friend the politician, have a delegation of politicians go out there with banners. Justice justice justice! In her thoughts she twisted and turned like a crazed woman in the middle of a street with traffic approaching on all sides. Friends did what they could, consoled, raged, sympathized: but no one, no one in the world could remedy what had been done.

She went to see a solicitor and as she sat there giving dates, facts, scraps of her married life, she had this certainty that what was happening was unreal and that presently someone would nudge her and laugh and say, 'It is all a game, we were just testing you.' But no. The interview went on. He was an old man, genial in a quiet way and a specialist in divorce. He looked down at his notebook when the time came to ask about infidelity. He had to know.

'Well yes,' she said.

'How many times?'

'Once?'

'Would you like to tell me how it happened.'

'No I wouldn't ...' she said as she began. She had stopped going to Confession but this was a return in memory to that ordeal and she blessed herself mentally but telling the story aroused no contrition just a bad taste. A night of tattiness. Absurd, to have to mention it at all.

'And you say your husband did not know about this.'

'No there is no connexion between the two events.' Ah, no, the retribution was far more hideous, far more comprehensive than that. Retribution for what! She talked calmly, sometimes looking at his face bent over the big notebook, sometimes at his good jacket draped on a spare chair. He wore a tattered jacket with leather patching on the elbows and had she known him better she would have made some nice comment about his prudence.

'Now your husband, this letter is a bit extreme ...' he said, scanning it again.

'He's like that,' she said. She had no wish to say much

else, no wish to list his failings or plead her case, these are things done in hope, in fury, and hope and fury expired days before. Even sitting there seemed pointless, absurd.

'Now tell me, since you left him, did he molest you?' The very question roused them both a little.

'No,' she said, shaking her head back and forth.

After he had taken all the information he closed the notebook and looked at her.

'What did you marry a man like that for?'

'It seemed to be what I wanted.'

'Marry a ...'

'I knew less then ...'

Although her face was to the window and light was pouring in on her there was no trace of tears or breaking down.

'Silly girl,' he muttered but in a way that was affectionate and not reprimanding. Then abruptly he asked if he might get her a brandy and she said 'no.' He looked at her hand on the desk, the fist clenched, veins showing through a density of freckles and slowly he put his own hand over hers and held it there.

'We'll do everything we can,' he said in a low voice.

She made no reply.

It boiled down to a question of money. They could go there, if she could afford it, they would fight it through the proper legal channels, but it would take time, a lot of time, a lot of money. He was an honest man, he was not going to tell her otherwise.

After a little while she rose and left, and down in the street a lull had occurred as if all the traffic had been suspended and rather boldly she crossed the road.

*

It took days to write, though the difficulty was not what to say, but how to say it. Her mind was made up, she had withdrawn. The odds were too great, the battle already won. She did not have his wickedness. She did not have his weapons.

She wrote:

Dear Eugene,

I have decided to let Cash stay with you for the time being. I trust that you will do everything for his well-being as I am sure you will. My solicitor will be in touch with you shortly.

Dear Cash,

My geography is not good. What is the latitude and longitude of where you are? What food do you eat? And what about your school? I expect it is all quite strange but no doubt very exciting. If you like I will send your comics.

Nothing else, nothing too close or too tender, or too hurtful. She had not the desire to say anything else. It was as if the decision itself had washed her clean, had emptied her of purpose.

Cash sent her a map of the island. It was drawn in ink on a paper napkin and then the napkin had been cut around the edge to the exact squat-bottle shape. Towns were marked and streams and a bread shop and a swimming pool and the sea at the bottom. There were hibiscus trees all over and these did not look like trees at all but like triangles of black in between the other features. At the top he had written in capital letters 'THE HEAVENS ARE BLUE'. When she looked at it she supposed that they had been eating in a restaurant, all three of them, and one of them had said her name and Cash had decided or had been prompted to do the drawing. She studied it very carefully so that she could make comments in her next letter. Also she had it pressed between two sheets of glass and used it as a sort of paper-weight. In the next letter she told him this and enclosed the comics. It would go on like that, letters back and forth over the years, photographs at intervals, and these she dreaded, and she knew that she would have to metal herself against them.

After Christmas Kate had herself sterilized. The operation was done by a private doctor and it entailed a short con-finement in an expensive clinic – money that might other-wise have been frittered on clothes or a summer holiday. On the second day Baba came to see her and found her sitting up in bed reading a newspaper article about women who for the purpose of scientific experiment had volunteered to spend a fortnight in an underground cave. Kate read: 'Doctors in touch by telephone from an adjacent cave con-tinue to be astonished at the physical resilience and lively spirits of the women who were unknown to each other before the vigil began.'

'Frank says you might as well move in with us ...' Baba said, interrupting. She had stopped calling him by the name of Durack.

'Really?' Kate said, pleased, surprised.

'He suggested it, not me,' Baba said, gruff.

'He usen't to like me,' Kate said.

'He must be getting over it,' Baba said but she was glad at being able to make the offer all the same. They would have each other, chats, their moments of recklessness, the plans that they'd both stopped believing in long ago.

'Well,' Baba said after some time, meaning: 'What does it feel like?'

'Well,' Kate said. 'At least I've eliminated the risk of making the same mistake again,' and for some reason the words sent a chill through Baba's heart.

'You've eliminated something,' Baba said. Kate did not stir, not flinch, she was motionless as the white bedpost. What was she thinking? What words were going on in her head? For what had she prepared herself? Evidently she did know for at that moment she was quite content without a qualm in the world. It was odd for Baba to see Kate like that, all the expected responses were missing, the guilt and doubt and sadnesses, she was looking at someone of whom too much had been cut away, some important region that they both knew nothing about.

...have each other, of ... romantic? I resolved that the
plants that thrived here, I'd be better up in ...
Will, let's talk about that little tree ... home.

Well, Rita said, *... and I was quite ... of*
taking the ... and ... and ... on the
weeks—and with the ...

... ultimate ... of ... that ...
... Rita ... she ... ... was the ...
... ... were ...
... ... herself. It ... ...
... ... was quite comfortable and
... the ... ... for Baba ... ... the
... the ... ... and
... ... She ... looking at ... of whom
... ... sense ... ... that
they both knew ...